THE RESCUE OF ELIZABETH BENNET

A PRIDE AND PREJUDICE VARIATION BOOK 2

BELLA BREEN

THE RESCUE OF ELIZABETH BENNET

Elizabeth will marry Mr. Collins even if Mrs. Bennet has to drag her to the altar.

When Mr. Bennet dies, Mr. Collins takes over Longbourn. He shows his true character when he vows to force the Bennets from their home unless he is given Elizabeth Bennet's hand in marriage.

Elizabeth, who has promised only to marry for love, refuses. But as her mother and sisters take increasingly drastic steps to force Elizabeth to wed, how long can she resist? Will Elizabeth make the ultimate sacrifice to save her family from being cast out?

Mr. Darcy fights his attraction to Elizabeth, but when he discovers Elizabeth is set to marry Mr. Collins, the next day, he must face his feelings before his love slips away. Can he rescue Elizabeth before it's too late? And if so, will the pair of them survive Mr. Collins' revenge?

The Rescue of Elizabeth Bennet is a 62,000 word, standalone damsel in distress novel with a guaranteed happily ever after.

Bella Breen

www.bellabreen.com

bellabreenbooks@gmail.com

Book Cover: Bella Breen

Editor: Rosie Steele

Proofreader: Lisa Hatfield

Created with Vellum

To Jay Machael.

To EAW, Echo, Mr. Sparkle, Pat, Brenda and Quinn who kept me working and sane in KWORKI.

To Kate McKeever who kept me sane in the real world.

To Lisa Hatfield who is the greatest proofreader and fan ever. To Dawn Erickson who had great developmental advice.

To all my readers who reviewed and commented, I love you!

I especially look forward to the comments from Gfrisby, Demelza, Lhatfield, nanciellen, mangosmum, Jansfamily4, Deanna27, Another Lizzie, nancy jeanne, SunriseImagination, LeslieE, cckeimig, Doris212, Avanell.

CHAPTER 1

Elizabeth Bennet stood in front of Netherfield Park and waited for the Bennets' carriage to pull around. She was quite sure that Mrs. Bennet had arranged for their carriage to come last, which did not make the Bingleys any fonder of the Bennets.

Elizabeth had a first-hand view of how much some Bingleys wanted them to leave. Mr. Bingley was still talking to Jane, completely oblivious to Caroline Bingley, Mrs. Louisa Hurst, and Mr. Hurst yawning, coughing and making pointed comments about how much they wanted to go to bed. This embarrassment on top of the entire mortifying and disappointing evening made Elizabeth wish she could fly home like a bird. Elizabeth was glad Jane and Mr. Bingley had this extra time to talk to each other, though. She was sure that Mr. Bingley would offer for Jane within a sennight.

However, that was the only thing Elizabeth was glad for this evening. She had spent extra time on her hair and dress to look good for George Wickham, who never even appeared at the ball. He had sent a word with his friend Denny that he decided it was best if he did not show up because of someone else there. Denny did not name anyone, but pointedly looked at Mr. Darcy.

So Mr. Darcy had ruined her evening without even trying. Then he had the gall to ask her to dance! This after he insulted her at the Meryton Assembly when he stated that she was not handsome enough to tempt him! Elizabeth did not care for men who could not make up their minds. She especially did not care for men who ruined the livelihoods of others. Namely how Mr. Darcy ruined George Wickham's life.

Charlotte Lucas had warned her not to make Mr. Darcy angry, that he was a man of great consequence. Charlotte was of course correct; however,

Elizabeth could not keep quiet about such injustices as Mr. Darcy did to poor George Wickham. During her dances with Mr. Darcy, she questioned him. It did not go well.

She left the dance more frustrated than ever with Mr. Darcy. She did not know nor care what Mr. Darcy thought of her. The man may have 10,000 pounds a year, but he lived in Derbyshire. How did his opinion even matter to her? He was just a friend of Mr. Bingley, an arrogant and proud friend.

Then the Bingley sisters had to stick their nose into it. Caroline told her that she did not know the particulars, but she was quite sure George Wickham had done something awful to Mr. Darcy. Did they not think that Mr. Darcy told them whatever would make him look good?

And then, to make the night even worse, Elizabeth had accidentally agreed to dance the first two with Mr. Collins. What an embarrassment! She blushed just remembering it. Mr. Collins did not even know how to dance correctly. He stepped on her feet, turned in the wrong directions and used her exceedingly ill. She could not wait to get away from him, but he continued to embarrass her, along with her entire family, except Jane, throughout the night.

Finally, the Bennets' carriage pulled up. If she had to listen to Miss. Bingley utter one more time how much she wished to go to bed, Elizabeth did not know what she would do. They all squeezed into the carriage with some of them sitting on each other's laps. And no, she would not sit on Mr. Collins' lap, thank you for the offer though.

She did not know how Mr. Collins ever came to be a parson. He was so entranced with the female figure. She pitied whoever had to marry him, for no one could stand his fawning behavior for long. She vowed to marry for love; nothing less than love, to a man that was intelligent, playful, and one that she respected.

~

Mr. Darcy did not feel that he had to stand with the Bingleys and wait for their last guests to leave, but for some reason he could not keep himself from the occupation. So, he stood quietly listening to the comments of Miss Bingley and Mrs. Hurst, the quiet talk of Mr. Bingley and Miss Bennet, and the simpering praises of Miss Bennet by Mrs. Bennet.

He had not thought his friend in danger until Mrs. Bennet had stated during the ball that she expected Mr. Bingley to offer for Miss Bennet soon. He then paid attention to his friend and Miss Bennet throughout the rest of the evening. He would much rather have kept an eye on those two, but the rest of the Bennet family, except Elizabeth, seemed determined to make spectacles of themselves. His attention was drawn to their lack of decorum over and over.

It was obvious that the Bennet family was an embarrassment. It was a miracle that Mr. Bingley chose to dance and talk to Miss Bennet, given the poor behavior exhibited by Mrs. Bennet, Miss Mary, Miss Catherine, Miss Lydia and even Mr. Bennet. There was no way he would let Mr. Bingley make such a monumental mistake and offer for Miss Bennet. Sure, Miss Bennet was nice and pleasing to look at, but her family was horrid. The younger girls, Lydia and Kitty, ran around and played as if a ball was a big lark for them. Mary Bennet could not understand that this was not her own theater to showcase her lackadaisical pianoforte talents. And that singing voice! Mr. Darcy shuddered.

He could not think of anything bad about Elizabeth, though. Her eyes, her pleasing form, her luscious lips. He had enjoyed holding her hand while dancing with her. Unfortunately George Wickham had told her a fictional version of events that Elizabeth believed. She had spent their dance questioning him. Of course she did not outright accuse him, but her questions were obviously about Wickham. Instead of being angry at Elizabeth, he was attracted even more to her quick mind. However, he was very angry at Wickham.

It was far too dangerous to pay any more attention to Elizabeth Bennet. He greatly admired her wit, intelligence, and pleasing figure, but it was too dangerous for him to continue to think of her, let alone be around her. He could not marry someone with such a family as hers. He would have to exert control on himself; the same control that he had put forth in every other aspect of his life. He would ignore the Bennets, especially Elizabeth Bennet, from this day forward.

CHAPTER 2

Elizabeth woke, not as was her custom, by the light of the sun, but by a scream. She looked into the darkness. What had she heard? Was that in a dream of hers? Then, she heard the scream again, a long-drawn-out keening.

She sat upright. That was no dream. What was wrong? Jane, who shared her bed, also sat straight up. "What was that?"

Elizabeth pulled off the covers and jumped out of bed onto the cold floor. "That sounds as if it is coming from inside the house!"

The loud keening started again. "I think... I think that is Mama!" Elizabeth grabbed the lamp by their door and walked out of the room. She ran down the hall to her parent's room. She passed the doors of her sisters' rooms. Her sisters were looking out of the open doorways.

Elizabeth knocked on her parent's door. "Mama? Mama! Is that you? What is wrong?"

There was no answer except for the continued wailing. Elizabeth opened the door and held up the lamp. Mrs. Bennet knelt on the bed, rocked back and forth, her face covered with her hands. Elizabeth walked over to the bed but could see nothing the matter.

She put her hand on Mrs. Bennet's back. "Mama? Are you having a nightmare? Why are you crying?"

Elizabeth saw more light enter the room. She turned to see Jane and her other sisters crowding into the room. Elizabeth looked back at the bed, planning to snap Mrs. Bennet out of her nightmare, when she glanced at her father's form in the bed.

Mr. Bennet was gray, his mouth hung open. Elizabeth raised her hand off her mother's back and covered her mouth. She backed up, shook her head and heard the loud keening sound again. It was not until she dropped to the floor that she realized the noise was coming from herself. Her father was dead. The father she loved, the parent most like her, the father she treasured was dead.

Someone took the lamp from her before it fell on the floor. Elizabeth sat back on her heels, rocked back and forth, and cried. It could not be true. This could not have happened. Her father could not be dead, but the crying and wailing confirmed that he had died.

Elizabeth stood with help from Jane. Kitty and Lydia held each other, cried, and stood covered with a blanket. Although tears ran down Mary's face, she was the only one that seemed to have a presence of mind as she directed their servant, Hill. Elizabeth glanced at her father and looked away as she cried in earnest again. It did not last long this time, as she was fresh out of tears. She had not thought it possible to have cried so much that she had no tears left.

The girls wrapped their mother in a blanket and took her downstairs to sit by the fire. She was still in shock and had not spoken a word. Soon, Mrs. Bennet would come back to be more like herself, but for now she was quiet.

Elizabeth stared down at her tea, unsure of what to even do. How did one go on without their favorite parent? How did one go---

"My word! I had been sleeping with stuffing in my ears as I always do, for it is so hard for me to get a good sleep without peace and quiet, but I heard the entire household in an uproar. Is this how you treat a guest trying to get sleep at night?"

Elizabeth turned and faced a new horror. Mr. Collins stood in the drawing room. Mr. Bennet had always teased the girls that whenever he died, Mr. Collins would turn them all out. And now, Mr. Bennet had died, and Mr. Collins was here. He would turn them all out. Not only would they no longer have a father, they would no longer have anywhere to live either.

Nobody spoke. Elizabeth was sure that no one wanted to tell Mr. Collins the news. The sooner Mr. Collins knew, the closer it came to the Bennets being thrown out. But being a parson, Mr. Collins surely would not do that? He would be kind, would he not?

Mrs. Bennet wailed and cried again. "Oh my poor, Mr. Bennet. You are gone now and Mr. Collins will turn us all out!"

Mr. Collins went white as a sheet. "What? Is that true? My cousin Mr. Bennet, he is dead?"

Elizabeth looked to Jane who looked to Mrs. Bennet. Mrs. Bennet was in no state to answer Mr. Collins.

Mary broached the subject at last. "Our father has died tonight, Mr. Collins."

Mr. Collins seemed shocked, and for that, at least, Elizabeth was glad to see. She had not thought Mr. Collins was a mercenary, that he would throw them out. She must have been wrong in her assessment of his character. Which reminded her of something Mr. Darcy had said earlier in the night. What a horrible night this was.

~

MR. DARCY WALKED to the dining room late the next day. He had the habit of getting up at a decent time in the morning. He would go over his letters, dictate business with the stewards at his different properties, and enjoy peace and quiet before the Bingleys rose. But the day after the ball, he allowed himself to sleep in.

"Good afternoon." He entered the dining room, famished.

Miss Bingley was, as usual, the first to respond to him. "How are you, Mr. Darcy? Did you sleep well after the long, long night?" Miss Bingley looked at her sister, Mrs. Hurst.

Mrs. Hurst nodded her head. "Oh yes, such a long night. I do not know why the Bennets had their carriage pulled around last so long after everyone else had left! No care for anyone else? We wanted to go to sleep."

"I slept quite well, thank you." Mr. Darcy drank his coffee.

"What did you think, Mr. Darcy?" Miss Bingley turned to her favorite subject.

"I am afraid I missed the question, Miss Bingley." Mr. Darcy did not even look at her.

"Of the Bennets leaving their carriage to be pulled last and so far after everyone else had left. Is that not a shameful display? An obvious attempt at match-making for Miss Bennet and Mr. Bingley?" Miss Bingley looked around the room, making sure again that her brother was not present.

"I care not to hear about the Bennets anymore. They displayed themselves last night in a wanton and a shocking lack of decorum and propriety."

Miss Bingley sat back in her chair with a smile. She looked at her sister Mrs. Hurst, who smiled back at her. Not only was Mr. Darcy over his fascination with Miss Elizabeth's fine eyes, but it seemed he disliked the entire family as well. Which was ideal for their plans.

"Do you think, Mr. Darcy, that my brother has gotten... quite close to Miss Bennet? What do you think of that?" Miss Bingley leaned forward and waited with bated breath for Mr. Darcy's answer.

"I find it alarming." Even though his answer was quite short, it was the exact sentiment that Miss Bingley shared.

"I agree with you completely, and so does Louisa."

Mrs. Hurst nodded. "Indeed. That family is shameful. I do love dear sweet Jane, but there is no possible way we can allow Charles to marry her. We need to talk him out of it."

CHAPTER 3

The Bennet family had come to terms with the fact they were down one member. Meryton's undertaker had taken Mr. Bennet's measurements and left. A coffin would be delivered soon, and then Mr. Bennet would lie in state in Longbourn before the funeral.

The Bennet women had mourning clothes, but they were not appropriate for mourning a close family member. They had gray and lavender dresses, not the black needed to sit with Mr. Bennet and attend his funeral. They could not leave the house, therefore they called the dressmaker from Meryton and ordered six dresses to be made with haste. The purchase bothered Elizabeth, as only Mr. Bennet had known their finances, but there was nothing to be done for it. They had to have proper mourning clothes.

Elizabeth walked to Mr. Bennet's study and sat in a guest chair before Mr. Bennet's desk. She could not go behind the desk and sit in Mr. Bennet's desk, but it was comforting to sit in his study. Who would take over the duties of minding the finances? How much money did their family even have? Did they have enough money to live in Longbourn, if Mr. Collins let them? If necessary, would they have enough money to move to a smaller house that was cheaper to live in?

Now that Mr. Bennet had died, would all the funds from the harvest go to Mr. Collins? These were questions that needed to be answered. She hoped that when the Gardiners arrived from London, Mr. Gardiner would go over their documents and tell them the status of their finances.

Aunt Phillips was with Mrs. Bennet in her bedroom. Mrs. Bennet was out of shock and now in her dramatic crying phase, as Mr. Bennet had labeled it. Elizabeth remembered how he had labeled each of Mrs. Bennet's different phases and they had shared a smile and a laugh. Elizabeth missed him dearly. Who else would laugh at the ridiculousness of life with her? No one else in the family shared their sense of humor.

~

THE NEXT DAY Mr. Bennet laid in state in Longbourn in a coffin lined with black bombazine. The Bennets wore black bombazine and crepe dresses with black ribbons. It was hard for Elizabeth to keep her spirits up. With them all wearing black and black on the windows, it was a dreary house.

Elizabeth and Jane took a break and walked the grounds of Longbourn. "I hope this will not prevent Mr. Bingley from visiting you, Jane?"

"I am sure Mr. Bingley will observe the proprieties. He will pay his respects."

Elizabeth hoped so. She had a feeling though, after observing the Bingleys at the Netherfield Ball, that the only one at Netherfield that still admired any Bennet was Mr. Bingley himself. She was sure that Miss Bingley and Mrs. Hurst would talk him out of coming to pay his respects at Longbourn. Poor Jane. It would be quite a sad revelation for her.

"How are you faring, Lizzy? I know Papa was your favorite, and you were his favorite."

"I have come to terms with it. We had always known someday he would die. With Papa so much older than Mama, I should have realized that it was not so far off. However, I did not expect it this soon. I thought we had at least another decade."

Jane squeezed Elizabeth's hand. "I wonder what caused it. The apothecary said nothing other than it was his heart."

Elizabeth shrugged. "I suppose we will never know. I am glad that Mr. Collins has said nothing about throwing us out."

Jane looked at her sister. "Elizabeth, I do not share your pessimism. Mr. Collins will say nothing about being master of Longbourn while we are in our period of mourning."

Elizabeth looked at Jane with exasperation. "Jane, you know I do not share your optimism in seeing the good in everyone. I believe I have a fair measure of Mr. Collin's character, and I fear he will not wait until we are out of mourning to tell us we have to leave our home."

"Lizzy, I fear you are much too hard on Mr. Collins. This must be a shock to him. His cousin just died."

"A cousin he had written once and visited right before he died. No, I do not think he has any fondness for us. Well, except for when he said he planned to marry one of us to heal the breach. I wonder if he will proceed with that plan."

Jane turned. "Again, I do not think he will do anything until we are out of our period of mourning. There is no need for you to worry, Lizzy. Indeed, I think you worry too much."

Jane and Elizabeth sat in the drawing room with Mr. Bennet in the coffin. They talked to their neighbors, the Lucases, when Elizabeth heard the unmistakable noise of a carriage pull up. Elizabeth was sure it was the Gardiners at last. She looked forward to a hug from her aunt and uncle. These last few days had been so hard to get through.

"Charlotte, if you will excuse me, I believe my relatives from London have just arrived."

Elizabeth walked out of the drawing room, eager to see the Gardiners. When the front door was opened by Hill, her smile dropped. It was Mrs. Hurst, followed by Miss Bingley, Mr. Bingley and Mr. Darcy. Elizabeth had not expected all of them, and she was not pleasantly surprised. No, in her time of mourning over her father's passing, she did not want to hear one word of contrariness. She had also had enough of Mr. Darcy at the Netherfield Ball. She had still not forgotten what George Wickham had told her about his treatment at Mr. Darcy's hands.

Mr. Bingley walked to Elizabeth with his hands out. "Miss Elizabeth, may you accept my condolences. It is so shocking. Why, I thought Mr. Bennet was in excellent health when I last saw him."

Elizabeth squeezed his hands. "Thank you, Mr. Bingley. That means a great deal. It was shocking as we thought he was in perfect health."

The Bingley sisters now surrounded their brother. Elizabeth did not want to be trapped in the hallway with them. "Please come into the drawing room."

She curtsied and turned down the hallway to her father's study. She knew she was being a coward, but she did not have the best control over herself right now. She knew how Miss Bingley and Mrs. Hurst antagonized her, to say nothing of Mr. Darcy.

CHAPTER 4

Mr. Darcy appreciated the form of Elizabeth Bennet as she walked away. He could not keep his eyes off her no matter how much he willed himself to do so. She drew his eyes like a moth to a flame. Now that she was out of sight, he sighed and flattened his lips. He had the distasteful task of being around the rest of the Bennet family, all of whom irritated him except for the eldest two.

But he had to do this because he planned to watch Miss Bennet's treatment of Charles. If she treated Charles the same as any other visitor, then they would need to have a talk with Charles. Yes, it was sad Miss Bennet's father had just died, but that was no reason for Charles to propose marriage to someone that did not love him. Mr. Darcy knew his friend fell in love at least six times a year. It was Mr. Darcy's job as a friend to keep Charles out of trouble.

The group walked into the drawing room with Mr. Bingley leading the way. He shared heartfelt condolences with Mrs. Bennet, who implored Mr. Bingley to sit near Miss Bennet on the sofa. Mr. Darcy watched Miss Bennet carefully. He saw her look up at Charles with a smile, but she gave no other sign that he was special to her.

Mr. Darcy stood back in a corner of the drawing room after he had uttered the most perfunctory of condolences to Mrs. Bennet. That seemed to be all right by her because she did not even thank him. Even at her husband's lying in state, Mrs. Bennet could not behave with good manners.

Miss Bingley soon joined him in the corner. "How long do you think we will have to stay? I loathe being around the Bennets longer than necessary. Do you think they will have our carriage leave last and after considerable delay?" Caroline laughed to herself.

Mr. Darcy did not respond. He felt Miss Bingley making sport of the family in mourning was in poor taste, no matter how much he did not like them. But he said nothing, for correcting Miss Bingley on her behavior was talking to a brick wall.

Mr. Darcy stared at Miss Bennet, who talked with Charles. One of the Lucas boys interrupted to pay his respects to Miss Bennet. Her facial expression was much the same as when she talked to Mr. Bingley. Mr. Darcy flattened his lips. No, it did not look like Miss Bennet cared more for Mr. Bingley than any other man.

Someone knocked him off balance by bumping into his left side. Mr. Darcy turned and found Mr. Collins, to his horror---the same man who had introduced himself at the Netherfield Ball, having not even been introduced previously. Mr. Darcy could not believe his aunt had hired such a foppish idiot to be parson of Hunsford, but she liked to be fawned over. However, Mr. Darcy did not.

"Mr. Darcy, it shows such Christian kindness for you to come and pay your respects to my dear cousin and his family, the Bennets. It shows such a conscientious Christian heart, such good character, the results of superb breeding, as your aunt and my patroness,

Lady Catherine de Bourgh would say. I am reminded---"

Mr. Darcy bowed and left the drawing room, unable to stand any more of this. He walked out the front door and climbed into the carriage. Mr. Darcy did not want to run into Miss Elizabeth in the house, and he knew she was fond of walking, so the carriage was the only safe place from her. He would never forget how she had looked after walking to Netherfield from Longbourn to take care of her sister. How beautiful her countenance was from the exercise; how bright her eyes were.

No, it was no good for him to think of that. He put a firm hold on those thoughts and pushed them aside. It would not do for Charles to marry into that family and it would not do for him, a Darcy, either. No matter how much a young woman might entice him with her body, and in this case her mind as well, his father had implored upon him the importance of marrying sensibly to carry on the Darcy name. Marrying into the Bennet family was not sensible at all.

Elizabeth sat in her father's study again. She could hear the noise from the drawing room, and though she felt guilty at not being there to help support her mother and sisters, she needed a break. There were only so many condolences and sad glances she could handle. It seemed everyone in Meryton knew their house had been entailed to Mr. Collins.

Mr. Collins acted like he was already in charge of Longbourn. He accepted condolences for his cousin, whom he had met not that long ago; ordered the servants about; and decided all parts of the funeral. He had even ordered the Bennet girls to be quieter with their voices and look more pleasing with their appearance. Elizabeth had looked to Mrs. Bennet for help, but she was still not quite herself.

The apothecary had come and given Mrs. Bennet laudanum so she could sleep through the night. Elizabeth knew her mother took some during the day as well, so Mr. Collins was running the house without any opposition. Elizabeth longed to tell him that their father was not even buried yet and Mr. Collins needed to give them time, but she did not want to anger the man who held their future in his control.

Elizabeth stood and walked over to her father's desk. She wished he had had the presence of mind to save money for them in case a son was never born, but he had not. Mrs. Bennet loved to spend, and Mr. Bennet did not like having friction in the house, so he gave in to whatever Mrs. Bennet wanted. Elizabeth was scared there was barely any money for them to live on. She did so wish that Mr. and Mrs. Gardiner would arrive soon. Elizabeth wanted Mr. Gardiner to go over their finances and tell them the truth of their situation.

She had another fear she did not want to admit or even think of. She knew Mr. Collins had mentioned marrying one of the Bennet daughters to heal the breach. Did he still plan to? Elizabeth hoped not. If he did, she was sure he would wed Mary. They were most alike in personality. That was the best outcome Elizabeth could hope for. It would be a trial to live with Mr. Collins at Longbourn, but at least they would have a home.

CHAPTER 5

On the day of their father's funeral, Elizabeth dressed in her black bombazine dress, making sure she looked perfect to honor Mr. Bennet. Down the hall, Mary said, "I shall hope we can still attend the Holiday Assembly in Meryton at the start of the new year. I would hate to miss playing the songs I have been practicing. We should be in half-mourning by then I am sure."

Elizabeth heard heavy footsteps in the hall which had to be their irritating cousin. "My dear cousin Mary, everyone would surely love to hear you play, as music is one of the ways to reach God and honor him. You are quite charitable in sharing your gifts with everyone, but I implore you not make plans past a few weeks. You shall not be long at Longbourn unless one of you girls marries me."

Elizabeth could not have heard her cousin correctly. She walked out of her bedchamber into the hall and faced Mr. Collins. "Mr. Collins, could you repeat that? I am not sure I heard you."

Mr. Collins walked out of Mary's doorway, bowed to Elizabeth, and stood up. "My dear cousin Elizabeth, you are such a sight for sad eyes. Your dear father, Mr. Bennet, I wish that he could be here himself. He would be so proud at how you favor him with your mourning attire."

"Mr. Collins, could you repeat what you said earlier about our being turned out of Longbourn?" Elizabeth had no patience for Mr. Collins' trait of long-winded, rambling sentences that carried next to no information.

"Oh, cousin Elizabeth, I do not wish to scare you or indeed any of the wonderful Bennet daughters, but I must have you out of Longbourn in a few weeks unless one of you makes me the happiest of men." Mr. Collins simpered at Elizabeth, who could no longer stand the sight of him. That proud, self-centered man forcing one of them to marry him or be responsible for their entire family being without a home!

Elizabeth turned and fled to Mrs. Bennet's bedchamber. It was time for her mother to stop subsisting on laudanum and bring her head into the world to stop Mr. Collins from throwing them all out. "Mama, talk sense into Mr. Collins. He says he will throw us out of our home in a few weeks if one of us does not marry him! Mama!"

She was too late as Mrs. Bennet had already taken a partial dose of laudanum, enough to get her through the funeral but not to put her to sleep. However, she was not fully aware of the surrounding activity. Blast that horrible man for giving them this ultimatum, this extortion on the day of their father's funeral and when their mother was incapacitated. Mr. and Mrs. Gardiner were at Meryton, having stayed at an inn, so Elizabeth could not share the horrible news until after the funeral.

There was one obstacle to doing just that, which was that Mr. Collins never left Elizabeth's side. He followed her everywhere, he sat next to her in the sitting room, he sat next to her in the church during the funeral. The only respite she received was when the men left to go into the cemetery for the burial.

Elizabeth walked up a pew and slid in next to Mrs. Gardiner, who was focused on consoling Mrs. Bennet, along with Aunt Phillips. Elizabeth bit her lip. She wanted to tell Mrs. Gardiner so they had a plan before Mr. Collins came back, or at least so her aunt could inform Mr. Gardiner, but she was loath to pull her aunt away from consoling her mother. Elizabeth was in shock from Mr. Collins' plans and could not spare any thought to how she missed her father. No, all her energy needed to be spent in finding a way out of Mr. Collins' horrible plans.

Jane slipped into the pew, sat next to Elizabeth, and held her hand. Elizabeth smiled, knowing Jane would help her tell Mr. Gardiner of the ultimatum from Mr. Collins and get him to look at their finances. Elizabeth had not gone into Mr. Bennet's study that morning to retrieve the financial papers since Mr. Collins had distracted her. She did not know how soon the Gardiners had to return to London, so time was of the essence. They had to know as soon as possible if the Bennets could afford to flout Mr. Collins and not have one sister marry him.

It was a rainy and overcast day for Mr. Bennet's funeral. The bells had rung recently, and even as far away as Netherfield, they could hear them. Mr. Darcy thought about Miss Elizabeth's eyes, her pleasing form, her intelligence and wit. What would happen to her now? He understood Longbourn to be entailed to that odious parson, Mr. Collins. Would he force them to move? Mr. Darcy shook his head. A parson forcing relatives out of their home after their father died? No, the Bennet family would have a house to live in. His aunt, Lady Catherine de Bourgh, would never have hired such a person.

Miss Elizabeth would be fine living in Meryton and marrying some local farmer. Mr. Darcy felt a pang in his chest at that thought, but he forced himself to ignore it. He could not consider that Bennet daughter a potential wife for himself. Her family's lack of manners and lack of connections could not be attached to the illustrious Darcy name.

Mr. Darcy turned from the window and studied the inhabitants of the sitting room. He caught Caroline studying him again. She was not even hiding her attempts at catching his eye. He flattened his lips and looked elsewhere in the room.

Mr. Darcy liked Charles like a brother, but his older sister was a headache. Mr. Darcy had always been an eligible bachelor with the Darcy name, the estate of Pemberley, and all the money that went with it. But he had never been in company with an eligible unmarried woman for as long as he had with Miss Bingley. Her obvious ploys had gotten on his nerves many times. If only there were some way to be around his friend Charles without his sisters.

"Dearest Louisa, shall we wager on the day the Bennets will leave Longbourn?" Caroline simpered and glanced up at Mr. Darcy, who turned his head in her direction.

"Oh, my yes, I think we shall. When did Mr. Bennet die? Oh yes, yes, just a few days ago therefore---"

Mr. Darcy left the sitting room with a barely audible "Excuse me".

The Bingley sisters stared at each other.

"Well, I give it six months before they are all turned out." Mrs. Hurst smiled and took up her embroidery.

"My dear brother, would you like to name the date when the Bennets will be turned out of their beautiful home?" Miss Bingley giggled to herself.

Mr. Bingley stood and approached Miss Bingley. "Caroline, that is inexcusable behavior. The Bennets have just lost their father. Why would you even think they would be turned out of their home?"

"Did you not hear the gossip, brother? Mr. Collins made the proclamation today. He will allow the Bennets to stay at Longhorn only if one daughter marries him. Otherwise they will be all thrown out."

Mr. Bingley stood with his mouth open, but he was the only one aghast at the news. "Thrown out? Are you sure that is the truth and not idle gossip?"

"Oh yes," replied Miss Bingley. "My maid told me just this morning. The whole family is in an uproar."

Mr. Bingley paled. "Does she know who Mr. Collins will choose? Surely not the eldest Bennet?" Miss Bingley slid her eyes to share a stare with her sister.

"No, Charles, I do not believe Miss Bennet was mentioned." Miss Bingley saw Mr. Bingley relax. She had to do something about this attraction he had to that Bennet girl. She liked Miss Bennet, but the rest of her family was horrible. Especially the upstart arrogance of Miss Bennet's younger sister, Miss Elizabeth.

Miss Bingley watched her brother leave the sitting room. She then shared a look with her sister. "Do you think he will call on Miss Bennet?"

"Oh, do not worry so, Caroline. It is the day of Mr. Bennet's funeral. No one can call."

Miss Bingley narrowed her eyes. "But he has continued to be infatuated with her. We have to do something."

CHAPTER 6

Mr. Bingley found Mr. Darcy playing pool in the game room. "Darcy, you left suddenly from the sitting room. I must apologize for my sister's behavior. That was awful of them to wager on when---"

Mr. Darcy stood up and held his hand out to stop Mr. Bingley speaking. "Please stop there, Charles. I have made a vow with myself not to hear anything else about the Bennet family." Mr. Darcy turned back to the billiard table and lined up another shot.

Mr. Bingley stared and blinked. "Upon my word! But why, Fitzwilliam? The poor family has just lost their father. I am concerned about---"

Mr. Darcy stood without taking the shot and turned around again. "Charles, I agree with you it is awful to lose one's parent, yet I cannot allow myself to think of the Bennet family any longer. Their lack of propriety and their want of decorum lead me to realize that they can have no future with me. Therefore, I will not allow myself to think of any one of them."

Mr. Darcy turned around and lined up his shot again. Enough time passed for Mr. Darcy to realize that Mr. Bingley would not speak up, and so he allowed himself to relax and take the shot. The three ball went into the corner pocket.

"You do not think the Bennets are good enough to associate with? They are of the gentry. They are landowners and Mr. Bennet is... was... a gentleman."

"Yes, from the strictest definition. But have you not seen the way the younger Bennet daughters act? Running about balls and assemblies, and stealing the soldiers' swords? Mrs. Bennet speaking with her mouth full, telling everyone she expects Miss Bennet to soon wed you? The entire family is a complete embarrassment. I give you the eldest Miss Bennet is an angel. But even Miss Elizabeth is contrary."

Mr. Darcy felt a pang in his chest as he said that last bit. He had lied about the beautiful Miss Elizabeth. It had been some time since he had thought of her as being arrogant, but he had to force himself out of his attraction to her somehow.

"Oh, I see." Mr. Bingley turned from Mr. Darcy and walked around the room.

Mr. Darcy bent over the table and lined up another shot. He felt bad for having broken Charles' heart, but it was necessary. It would be much easier for Charles to handle not marrying into a family with a complete lack of propriety than to be told that Miss Bennet did not like him the same.

LONGBOURN LOOKED sad with black in the windows. Elizabeth wiped away a tear that ran down her face. She had to be strong until she could figure a way out from the ultimatum Mr. Collins had delivered. Once they were secure, then Elizabeth would allow herself to mourn. Not only did she worry about their finances and future living arrangements, but she was spent and tired of moving around during the walk back to Longbourn to avoid Mr. Collins.

Elizabeth hung up her spencer jacket and walked into the dining room. Mrs. Bennet sat in her usual position, but Mr. Gardiner was now seated in Mr. Bennet's place as head of the family.

Mr. Collins walked into the dining room and stopped. "Pardon me, but as you must know, Longbourn was entailed to me. Since, Mr. Bennet is now dead, Longbourn is mine, and as such, I will be seated at the head of the table."

All of them turned to Mr. Collins with varying countenances. Mr. Bennet had only just been buried, and already Mr. Collins was asserting himself. Elizabeth's hands shook, rattling the cup she held against its saucer. Jane pulled Elizabeth's hand down and held it.

"Mr. Collins, I understand Longbourn has been entailed to you, but could you not allow things as they are to let the Bennets get used to being without their father?" Mr. Gardiner stood as he finished stating his request.

A smiling Mr. Collins looked around the room. "The Bennets are already aware I am in charge of Longbourn now, but I am not without generosity, for I am a Christian and am conscientious where it is needed.

The Bennets may live at Longbourn past a few weeks as long as one girl marries me." Mr. Collins bowed to Mr. Gardiner, whose mouth was open.

Mr. Collins stepped closer to Mr. Gardiner and used his body to push him away from the chair at the head of the table. Mr. Gardiner stepped away from Mr. Collins, who sat down and smiled benevolently at the shocked countenances at the table.

"This is most unusual---" Mr. Gardiner tried to implore to Mr. Collins' sensibilities, but that ended abruptly.

"If you could please sit, Mr. Gardiner. I own Longbourn now, and I shall sit at the head of the table, which is my place by right of entail."

"You cannot sit there, that was Papa's place! Mr. Gardiner sits there now!" Lydia's outburst showed a lack of decorum, and yet Elizabeth was pleased by it. She glanced at Mr. Collins to see him turn a most interesting shade of vermillion.

"As master of Longbourn I consider it one of my duties to instill proper decorum and propriety in young ladies that have been let run wild. Yes, I shall curb your displays, cousin Lydia. Take heed you do not draw my ire." The candlelight flickered off Mr. Collins face, casting a hideous caricature.

Mrs. Bennet cried. Mr. Gardiner, owning both decorum and propriety, considered the best course of action was to accommodate Mr. Collins. Those on that side of the table stood and moved one place down so that Mr. Gardiner sat next to Mr. Collins, protecting Mrs. Gardiner from Mr. Collins.

Dinner was served with no conversation except for Mr. Collins' oration on the wonderful funeral sermon and the changes he planned for Longbourn. The long stares and gasps passed his notice. The Gardiners held each other's hands to keep themselves from breaking propriety and throwing Mr. Collins out of his own house.

Once dinner was over and they were all in the drawing room, Mr. Gardiner opened the conversation. "Mr. Collins, you cannot very well mean to place the Bennet family, who so recently lost their beloved Mr. Bennet, out of their home with no resources. I cannot see a man of cloth pursuing that path, especially with a good living at Hunsford."

"Mr. Gardiner, it is so charitable for you to consider the future of the Bennet family. That is a kind and noble sentiment to consider those less well off than those of us that consider our means before spending."

Elizabeth ground her teeth to keep herself quiet.

Mr. Collins was not done speaking though. "But I am the master of Longbourn now, and my patroness Lady Catherine de Bourgh wants me marry as soon as possible. In fact, she stated that was the reason for my coming to Longbourn in the first place. She told me I must marry, and I must marry a good, sensible woman---"

"Mr. Collins, your patroness Lady Catherine de Bourgh is not here at Longbourn. When you move into Longbourn, you will no longer be parson of Hunsford. Why would you leave your parish with a good living and a noble patroness? At least let the Bennets have a longer amount of time before they need to find housing."

Mr. Collins' eyes bulged from his vermillion face. He sat up in the armchair almost as if it were a throne. "Mr. Gardiner, as you are related to the Bennets, I will try to be kind though you have overstepped your boundaries! I alone will decide on the running of Longbourn and I alone have a say over what shall be done. As I mentioned earlier, the Bennets will have several weeks to find housing if, I am not cold hearted, one daughter marries me. Except now the Bennets will have even less time, a few weeks, before they need to leave for new homes. I am not one to have my decisions questioned."

Elizabeth sat back in horror. Now they had less time? Elizabeth stared at Jane, who stared at Mr. Collins, her face blanched of all color. Elizabeth turned back to Mr. Collins. She wanted to ask why he was doing this to them; was he punishing them for the fight between Mr. Bennet and Mr. Collins? However, she was more afraid of decreasing their time at Longbourn even more if she questioned him. The odious clown had turned into an evil dictator.

"Mr. Collins!" Mr. Gardiner said. "You only gave them a few weeks before, and now you have made it even less? Do you feel that is the Christian thing to do? Would your patroness Lady Catherine de Bourgh be proud of what you are doing? That you are throwing a good family out of their house with no support?"

Mr. Collins narrowed his eyes at Mr. Gardiner. "You are not related to Mr. Bennet, you are Mrs. Bennet's brother, correct?"

Mr. Gardiner looked at his wife, then back at Mr. Collins, and nodded.

"I must ask you to leave."

Elizabeth could not hold back her gasp as she had not thought of her aunt and uncle ever being thrown out by Mr. Collins. How would Mr. Gardiner look over their finances now? She would not trust Mr. Collins to do it for them. No, she would expect that Mr. Collins would be less than honest, though he was a parson.

Elizabeth stood. "Mr. Collins, please, they are our relatives giving us solace in our time of need. Can you please let them stay here with us? Mr. Gardiner still needs to go over our finances, so we know how much we have at our disposal. Mr. Bennet has always used a shorthand he said other businessmen could understand. I fear my uncle is the only one with the ability to decipher Papa's notations." Elizabeth hoped her lie regarding her father using shorthand would allow the Gardiners to get access to the financial records and also prevent Mr. Collins from investigating them himself.

Mr. Gardiner stood. "You cannot plan to do this, Mr. Collins. We are here to give solace to the Bennet family, including my sister Mrs. Bennet. Come now, you cannot mean to turn them out a few weeks after they buried Mr. Bennet."

Mr. Collins stood from his armchair. "You will need to leave, Mr. and Mrs. Gardiner. You are not welcome at Longbourn anymore."

CHAPTER 7

Most of the family stayed away from Mr. Collins the rest of the day. Mary did not let Mr. Collins' actions keep her away, as she had always admired him. The rest of the Bennets were upstairs in their own bedrooms or with Mrs. Bennet, as they cried and commiserated on how horrible things had gone since Mr. Bennet died. They missed Mr. Bennet, but their main concern was to survive their cousin, Mr. Collins.

In their bedroom, Elizabeth brought up a subject she hoped would not upset Jane. "The best thing we have going for us is Mr. Bingley's attention to you. I hope he does not keep our state of mourning from offering for you."

Jane looked up at Elizabeth. "I do not know, Lizzy. He is a very conscientious man with good manners. I do not think he will offer for me while I am in mourning."

Elizabeth frowned. "That odious Mr. Collins! I never thought he would be this bad. Why could he not have been a simple-minded clown? Where did this greed come from?"

"We need to know what our finances are. I wish Papa had taken into confidence one of us such as you Lizzy, or at least Mama."

Elizabeth laughed. "Oh Jane, you know Mama would have spent all the money. She has never been one for figures. I think it was right that Papa not keep financial confidence with Mama, but he should have let one of us know. Especially, now that he is gone." Elizabeth choked on that last word.

Jane leaned over and hugged Elizabeth.

Elizabeth leaned back. "I have an idea. Instead of going to church, I will claim I am too ill to get out of bed. Then, when you have all left for church, I will go outside and through the window climb into the study and retrieve the financial papers. We will then send them to our uncle."

"That is a risky scheme, Lizzy. Why do you not do this before we leave for church? Go into the study in the night's middle and retrieve the papers, and then I can give them to Mr. Gardiner after church."

"That is a brilliant plan, Jane. Mr. Collins is such a sound sleeper I should have no problem staying undetected."

~

Elizabeth hid her wind-up clock under her pillow so it would not be loud when it went off. Unfortunately, she had been too nervous and the ticking too loud for her to get any sleep. When the alarm went off, Elizabeth crept through the cold house, out the back door, and around the side of the house to the study's window. She had left a copper tub hidden behind the bushes earlier in the day. Elizabeth turned the tub over, stood on it and pushed the window open before climbing through.

Since there was not much moonlight, Elizabeth lit the oil lamp. She turned it down so there was just enough light for her to see by. She had a shock when she saw the top of Mr. Bennet's desk. There was nothing on it. All the papers that had been there were gone.

"Oh no. Were had they gone? Did Mr. Collins take them?" All her hopes had rested on retrieving those financial papers.

Elizabeth tried all the drawers of the desk, but someone had locked them. She was so frustrated she rested her head on top of the desk and shed a few tears. Blast that Mr. Collins!

Elizabeth doused the lamp, climbed out of the window, and then closed it again. She carried the copper tub with her back into the house. It was no good to leave evidence behind. Her next plan of action was to get the keys from Mr. Collins. He was the one that had locked all the papers in the desk. Or he had taken the papers and right now was in the process of adding up the Bennets' money.

"ELIZABETH? ELIZABETH, WAKE UP."

Elizabeth rolled over and opened her eyes to see Jane lean over her.

"Did you get the papers?"

Elizabeth was filled with disappointment as she shook her head. Jane's countenance fell. "Nothing?"

"No papers were on top of the desk, and someone had locked all the drawers."

Jane groaned and laid back in bed. "I was so sure you could get them. What will we do now?"

"That is what I asked myself last night. We have to tell our uncle, Mr. Gardiner. He has to come to Longbourn, and Mr. Collins has to let him into the study so he can analyze the financial papers for us."

Jane looked over at Elizabeth. "How can he do that, since Mr. Collins banished him from Longbourn?"

"Mr. Collins is not behaving in the manner of a gentleman. I do not think Mr. Gardiner has to do anything Mr. Collins says. Mr. Gardiner is the head of our family now, not Mr. Collins."

"Do you think Uncle would agree? Will he come to Longbourn?"

"Jane, I do not know, but we have to try. We cannot leave to go to the local law firm or to anyone for help because we are in mourning. I hope the Gardiners have not left Meryton yet."

The Bennet family walked to church on Sunday in a curious manner. They tried to walk a distance away from their cousin Mr. Collins, even Mary as Lydia and Kitty bullied her. However, he would not allow them to walk several feet behind him, instead stopping and waiting for them to catch up. Having become wise to what they attempted, he put his hand under Mrs. Bennet's arm to escort her to church.

It was a sad family that walked into the church without their beloved father and an odious caricature in his place. When they entered the church, Elizabeth and Jane were gratified to see that the Gardiners were present. As a matter of fact, the Gardiners scooted over in their pew to make room for the Bennets to sit with them. Mr. Collins however did not want to be near the family he had thrown out of Longbourn. He walked Mrs. Bennet forward to the first pew. The Bennet daughters had to follow.

Elizabeth stared at the church's parson and hoped some of his decency would work its way into their cousin's pea brain. It was not a charitable thought at all, but Elizabeth did not care. What their cousin had done so far at Longbourn was inexcusable.

After service, the parishioners stood in front of the church and shared condolences and sympathies with the Bennet family. Mr. Collins could not force them away from that. As Mr. Collins told the parishioners how much he missed his wonderful cousin Mr. Bennet, Elizabeth rolled her eyes and slipped away to the Gardiners.

"Elizabeth, tell us, how are you? Mr. Collins does not seem a man that tends towards compassion and generosity." Mr. Gardiner looked very concerned for the health of the Bennets, but especially for Elizabeth, who was the Bennet most likely to stand up against Mr. Collins.

"I do not know how much time I have. We need you at Longbourn. I cannot find Papa's financial papers. We do not know how much money we have, or if we can afford to leave Longbourn and live in a small house... or if one of us has to marry him."

Mr. Gardiner nodded just as Elizabeth heard Mr. Collins call. "My dearest cousin Elizabeth? Where has she gone to this time? It is time for us to leave."

Elizabeth stared at the Gardiners and then walked back to where the rest of the Bennet family stood, huddled away from Mr. Collins.

"My dear cousin," Mr. Collins said, "you must stay with your family in trying times such as these to console with each other. This is no time for you to take off in glad talk and amusements. Why, your father has just been buried. Do not do it again."

Elizabeth ground her teeth as Mr. Collins turned and led the way back to Longbourn. She hoped Mr. Gardiner would find a hidden account full of money for them. She would miss Longbourn as it had been her only home, but she would not miss the toad that was owner of her home.

CHAPTER 8

Dinner after church was like the other meals since Mr. Bennet died and Mr. Collins took over Longbourn. Mr. Collins sat at the head of the table and pontificated on everything. Only Mary liked these meals as she quoted from the Bible and other religious books. Elizabeth found that she could not stomach to eat much with Mr. Collins at the head of the table.

After the meal Elizabeth would rather have gone upstairs or anywhere away from Mr. Collins, but she stayed in the drawing room and awaited her aunt and uncle's arrival. Where were they?

"My cousin Elizabeth, that is a fine embroidery you have there," Mr. Collins said. "Such fine stitching. It reminds me greatly of the embroidery Lady Catherine de Bourgh stitched herself as a young lady. Yes, she told me she had always been proficient with the needle. It is a disappointment that her daughter, Anne de Bourgh, does not have the same skill as her mother. I have always said needlework is a great pastime for a young woman of virtue. That and reading the Scriptures---"

Elizabeth was saved from another pontification of Mr. Collins by the tingling of the bells at the front door. Only Elizabeth and Jane were not surprised when Hill announced the Gardiners. The rest of the Bennets looked at Mr. Collins for they had all heard him banish their relatives from Longbourn. Mr. Collins' countenance was darkening to a shade not unlike a ripe tomato.

Elizabeth stood quickly. "It is good to see you again, Uncle---"

"Might I remind you I told you not to come here, yesterday? I will not allow you to---"

Elizabeth turned to her cousin. "Mr. Collins, they are our aunt and uncle. Surely you cannot send away relatives offering solace in our time of need."

Mr. Collins straightened his stance in front of the fireplace. "I can see, my dear cousin Elizabeth, that you are quite an innocent, as befits an unmarried woman of virtue. You are not yet wise to the ways the world as I am, being a parson and knowing the sins of my parish. And I know that Mr. and Mrs. Gardiner are not here to provide solace and comfort. No, they are here to drive a wedge between us to break up this family---"

Mr. Gardiner had heard enough. "Mr. Collins, I must insist! There are legal documents and financial papers that the Bennets have asked me to go over with them. As Mr. Bennet's brother-in-law, I have a duty to look after his family. Now, may I have access to Mr. Bennet's study?" Mr. Gardiner stood upright and stared at Mr. Collins, who at the moment greatly resembled a toad puffing up.

"You may not have access to anything at Longbourn! I am the owner of Longbourn; it has been entailed to me. You do not have access to anything, and I can provide all the information of legal affairs and finances for the Bennets." Mr. Collins stood proudly in the middle of the drawing room.

Mr. Gardiner was not one to give in to bluster. "On this point, I will have to disagree, Mr. Collins. I have a copy of my brother-in-law's will. A will which does reference the entailment of Longbourn. The will clearly states that I am to look after his family. One of the items so directed to me, as executor of his will, is to reconcile his finances and any items that do not get passed to your ownership with the entailment." Mr. Gardiner had pulled out the legal documents from his coat pocket and now proceeded to read from one. "You sir, are entitled to the house, the land, and the revenue generated by the lands after the death of Mr. Bennet. I believe you have a copy of this document, Mr. Collins?"

Elizabeth's lips twitched as she contained her smile. She glanced at Mr. Collins, who had clearly not expected to be confronted with facts.

Mrs. Bennet rushed to her brother, waving her handkerchief. "Oh, dear brother! Oh, thank you! You are doing right by my Mr. Bennet." Mrs. Bennet was overcome by tears.

Mr. Gardiner wrapped his arm around Mrs. Bennet's shoulder. "There, there sister. All will soon be put to rights. As soon as Mr. Collins lets me in the study, I will go over the finances." Mr. Gardiner looked up at Mr. Collins. "Mr. Collins? Will you open the study for me so that I may do my legal duty as executor of Mr. Bennet's will?"

Mr. Collins eyes darted around the room and saw that no one was looking upon him with favor. He nodded his head towards Mr. Gardiner and led the way to the study. Mrs. Bennet, Elizabeth, and Jane followed Mr. Gardiner into the room, but Mr. Collins stepped in front of Mrs. Bennet. "My dear Mrs. Bennet, a man's study with figures and finances is no place for the gentle mind of a woman." Mr. Collins then gave a perfunctory bow and closed the door; however Elizabeth's shoe was in the way.

"Pardon me, Mr. Collins, but since I helped Papa with the figures of the harvest for the last several years, I feel I could provide help to my uncle in locating the financial papers." Elizabeth looked her cousin in the eye, not cowed in the slightest by his glare.

Mr. Gardiner came back to the door. "Mr. Collins, as the finances do pertain to the Bennet family, I do not think you should bar them from this room or keep the information from them."

Mr. Collins darted his eyes around the room and twitched his lips. He moved towards the door, but again Elizabeth stopped him. "Mr. Gardiner, are the desk drawers locked? If they are locked, I believe Mama has the key."

Mrs. Bennet shook her head. "Oh no, Mr. Bennet always had the key for his desk."

Mr. Collins patted his jacket and then walked behind the desk. "I believe I may have the key. It is much safer to have a desk locked than unlocked." Mr. Collins proceeded to unlock every drawer. Elizabeth shared a look with Jane.

After Mr. Collins left the study, Elizabeth was happy to find all the financial papers in the drawers. Mr. Collins must have locked them to prevent his uncle's family from accessing them. His contrariness towards his own relatives continued to shock Elizabeth. How could someone so greedy be a parson?

Mr. Gardiner looked at the journals and papers and sighed. "This will take a good amount of time. Would you have a pot of tea sent in? I am sure you can find a better way to spend the day than in here watching me put a quill to paper."

Elizabeth laughed. "Me? I do not think he finds me companionable. I think he will choose Mary. They have common interests with sermons, lectures, and music. But I do hope it will not come to that. Mr. Gardiner will tell us if we have enough money to live on our own."

"Do you think that is possible, Lizzy? That Papa set aside money?" Elizabeth was not good at covering up her emotions and Jane, being her sister, knew how to read her. "Oh, I see. It is not good then. "

Elizabeth turned to Jane. "It might not be that bad. I do not know. We should wait to hear from Mr. Gardiner before we fret any further."

CHAPTER 9

Mr. Gardiner spent hours with the papers and journals Mr. Bennet had left behind. He checked his figures and then asked Hill to call Mrs. Bennet and the eldest Bennets into the study.

"Dear brother, tell me we will not be turned out on the streets penniless?"

Mr. Gardiner gazed at his sister, who had always been prone to dramatics. "Francine, take command of yourself." Mr. Gardiner took a deep breath and looked at his late brother-in-law's family. "I have gone through the financial and legal documents. What was purchased for Longbourn after Mr. Bennet inherited it and does not pertain to generating an income or care of the estate is yours. The money that is left from this year's harvest is a good ---"

Mrs. Bennet leaned back in her chair and waved her hands. "Oh, dear brother! How wonderful! We are saved! We are saved! We will have enough money to live on and no one will have to marry Mr. Collins. Now, I can---"

Mr. Gardiner's countenance was not one of joy when he interrupted his sister. "Francine, I fear you have received the wrong impression. I was not done with the particulars. The harvest was good, but the profit is such that there is little money left for you to live on, I am afraid. According to the entailment a certain amount needs to be set aside for the estate and the rest may go to Mr. Bennet's family. I am quite sorry, but the amount left is not enough for you to even rent a small house without finding employment."

A moment of silence and then Mrs. Bennet wailed. "How can this be? Were we not careful with our money? Surely there must be some mistake! How shameful to leave a widow and five daughters without any living."

Jane placed her hand on Mrs. Bennet's shoulder. "Mama, I am sure Mr. Gardiner was very thorough with his calculations."

"Indeed, I was. These calculations should also be verified by the solicitor in Meryton though." Mr. Gardiner's pronouncement was lost in the tears and wailings of his sister.

"That odious Mr. Collins! To come here and throw us out of our home, to leave us destitute without anything to our names. I would not want to live in a house torn away from a grieving family!"

"Mama! It is an entailment, there is nothing we can do."

"My dear sister, keep your voice down. It is all perfectly legal and within his rights, though it is not the Christian thing to do, nor will it make many friends among society when they hear of it."

"Do you know what he is planning to do? He will throw us out on the steps unless one of my dear girls marries him!" Mr. Gardiner nodded; he had already heard this news previously. Mrs. Bennet's recollection must have been dulled due to the laudanum she had been taking.

Elizabeth's mind was dulled because of the unexpected and unfortunate news. She had been sure there was enough money for them to live on. Even if they had to take a smaller house, she had never expected that they would still have to find employment. "What do you think are our chances are of marrying well with this news?"

Mr. Gardiner looked at Elizabeth. "I do think you would get a better answer if you asked your aunt instead of me. However, there are many respectable men that are employed and would make fine husbands."

Elizabeth blushed as she realized she had insulted her favorite uncle. "Oh, please pardon me, Uncle, I meant no offense---"

Mr. Gardiner smiled and raised his hands. "Elizabeth, I understand what you meant. This is a highly emotional time for us all."

There was no use lingering in the study any longer, for Mrs. Bennet continued to wail and cry no matter how Jane and Elizabeth tried to calm her.

~

ONCE MRS. BENNET was settled in her bedchamber, she asked Hill to bring Mrs. Gardiner. The younger Bennet girls also followed their aunt into the bedchamber.

"Mama, are we all saved then? We will not have to live with our horrible cousin?" Lydia said with no concern for being quiet.

"Lydia!" Elizabeth stared at her younger sister, but Lydia thrust her chin out and stared right back.

Mrs. Bennet wailed and fluttered her handkerchief. "Oh Madeline, my brother has told us Mr. Bennet did not leave enough money for us. We shall be thrown out, forced to be employed for a living unless one of my girls marries that odious man!"

Mrs. Gardiner sat down next to Mrs. Bennet, who was lying on her chaise. "Now calm yourself, Francine. I am sure there is much that can be done with the amount of funds you have left."

"But we are to be turned out unless someone marries that horrible Mr. Collins! This cannot be legal!" Mrs. Bennet was too distressed to listen to reason.

Jane sat down next to their aunt. "Mr. Gardiner said that we do not have enough money to leave Longbourn unless we were employed. If we did leave and were employed, what would the chances be for our making a good marriage?"

Mrs. Gardiner looked at the eldest Bennet girl, beautiful and sweet-natured Jane. It was a sad circumstance that Mr. Bennet had not thought more carefully of his family of five girls and saved money for this occasion. "I imagine you and Lizzy would be able to find respectable employment as governesses or companions. You would not be living together in the house with the rest of your family though. As for the younger girls..."

Mrs. Gardiner trailed off and looked at Lydia and Kitty, who were fighting over a black ribbon that Lydia had pulled out of Kitty's hair. Then she looked at Mary who sat apart from the others. Mrs. Gardiner turned back to Jane. "I believe Mary could find employment as a musical teacher. But from what I understand, your education has been left to each individual?"

Jane nodded and straightened a fold of her dress. "Yes. We are not so well educated as others."

"What my sister is trying to say," said Elizabeth, "is that we are prepared for nothing except getting married."

Their parents had never taken them to task to learn skills or languages like other society families such as the Longs and the Lucases. The Bennet girls could do whatever they wanted and therefore had not much to benefit themselves except their looks and charm. That would have been enough except in this circumstance, for now, unless one of them married Mr. Collins, they would all have to find employment.

"There are no relations on Mr. Bennet's side that could take some of you in?"

Jane and Elizabeth shook their heads. "The only relation is the one downstairs threatening to turn us out in a few weeks."

Elizabeth loved her father, but at this point in time, she could have thrown a book at him. She had not known they had so little money. If only Mrs. Bennet and Lydia could have curtailed their spending, maybe they would not have ended up in this predicament. But it was too late now. Mr. Bennet was dead and buried and Mr. Collins had taken over Longbourn.

CHAPTER 10

Mr. Bingley could not sit still. He was worried, and he did not like to be worried. Especially regarding that beautiful eldest Bennet girl that he could not get out of his mind. "Caroline, have you heard anything else about the Bennet family situation? I am most concerned about Miss Bennet."

Caroline shared a look with her sister Louisa, who had been practicing the pianoforte before her brother spoke. "What other news should I have heard, Charles?"

Caroline did not want her brother to be associated with the Bennet family. The only tolerable person was the eldest girl. The rest of the family was a nightmare except for the second-eldest, but her attitude was not the best.

"Whether the information you heard before was wrong? That they are to be thrown out of their house by their cousin unless one of the Bennet girls marries him?" Mr. Bingley stood in front of Caroline, who sat on the sofa.

"I have not heard anything that is contrary to the earlier news." Caroline drank her tea. She had heard that Mr. Collins had asserted himself as the new owner of Longbourn and was not pleasant anymore. Caroline would not wish Jane to have to marry him at all, but it was better than her marrying Charles.

Mr. Bingley took a few nervous breaths, walked a few paces and then turned back to face Caroline. "I suggest we go to Longbourn and pay them a visit. Bring up their spirits. They are in mourning, and it has to be incredibly difficult to lose their father. I cannot believe their cousin would be so cruel as to have them moved out of the house in a few weeks. I need to verify this for myself."

He smiled at his sisters and hoped one of them would be agreeable to the idea. He did not want to go to Longbourn by himself as that would be giving the wrong impression. Though he would like to marry the eldest Bennet, it was not done while a family was in mourning.

Caroline shrugged and looked at Louisa. "I would not mind paying Miss Bennet a visit. Would you, Louisa? I am curious to see if what I have heard about Mr. Collins' behavior is accurate."

Louisa nodded. "Me too. It would be a nice diversion on such a boring day."

Mr. Bingley flattened his lips but did not censure his sisters for their lack of Christian charity for those in mourning. He wanted them to go with him, so he called for the carriage to be readied.

Mr. Bingley knew better than to ask Mr. Darcy if he would want to go with them. Mr. Darcy had kept to his vow and left the room or changed the conversation anytime a mention of the Bennet family occurred. Mr. Bingley shook his head. Embarrassing family relations were no reason to turn aside a perfectly wonderful woman.

THE BINGLEY FAMILY was welcomed into the sitting room, where they found Mr. Collins seated closest to the fireplace. He stood and bowed, then resumed his seat in the largest armchair in the room.

Conversation was not forthcoming from any of the Bennets, or Bingleys as Mr. Collins immediately monopolized all conversation. "It is very kind of you to visit us, Mr. Bingley and your dear sisters. I find it is a Christian activity, visiting those who have recently lost a family member. It is an activity that I find myself having to do more often than not as parson of the Hunsford parish. I have quite a good living there. Yes, I have been fortunately blessed at my young age thanks to my patroness Lady Catherine de Bourgh." Mr. Collins paused to nod his head in deference to his currently not present patroness.

"Your living at Hunsford Parish is a valuable position," said Elizabeth, "and I question whether you could be angering your patroness by moving into Longbourn. Should you not be with your parish instructing your parishioners?" Elizabeth spoke with some embarrassment due to their company, but she was determined to find a way out of their situation.

"Why, my dear cousin Elizabeth, your concern for me regarding my patroness is insightful and caring of you. Yes, you are very thoughtful. But do not tax yourself as Lady Catherine de Bourgh knows that my cousin, your wonderful father Mr. Bennet, has recently expired. She stated right before I came for my visit that I must marry and marry quickly. After my cousin's sad passing, I received a letter from my bishop, forwarded from my parsonage by my housekeeper, expressing his condolences and assuring me that I can stay at Longbourn and that he will find a curate for Hunsford that I may guide and give advice to for the care of my parish." Mr. Collins ended his long speech with a large smile and nod to the well-dressed guests.

This revelation by their cousin was unexpected and unwelcome to the elder Bennets. With Mr. Collins having been granted permission to stay at Longbourn and manage Hunsford parish from afar, Elizabeth's plan had completely fallen apart. Her chance to convince Mr. Collins of his duties to his parishioners was gone. By sending that letter, the Bishop had further solidified the Bennets' fate. Elizabeth looked down at her hands with slumped shoulders. She was at a loss for other alternatives to their dire predicament.

Mr. Bingley cleared his throat. "That is quite surprising. I would think you would not want to stay here in Meryton away from your patroness, the one that asked you to marry quickly. Is that still an order of hers?"

"Such concern for your fellow man; you have such good breeding. I do plan to write Lady Catherine de Bourgh as often as I can, as well as the Hunsford curate, yet Longbourn is now my home. I do plan to marry quickly, as an estate needs a wife to manage it. And what better wife than one of the women who have lived here their whole lives?" Mr. Collins smiled and nodded at Elizabeth, to her horror.

The Bingley sisters hid their smiles at the good fortune that the gossip was true, however their brother blanched and stared at Jane. Only propriety kept him from standing up and declaring himself to Miss Bennet.

Elizabeth's only good thought came from knowing that in a few weeks they would be away from Mr. Collins. Employment as a governess or companion was much preferable to spending even a fortnight with that man. Elizabeth opened her eyes and glanced at Jane, who also sat with slumped shoulders, looking down. The only solution left for the Bennets was for Mr. Bingley to offer for Jane, but a glance at Mr. Bingley's countenance showed nothing but distaste. Elizabeth feared he was not a strong enough man to go against society's dictates and ask Jane to marry him so soon after their father died.

Elizabeth glanced at the Bingley sisters and wished she had not. They were barely trying to hide their joy at Mr. Collins' pronouncement. The visit ended quickly, as what could be said after such a pronouncement? Elizabeth was not one to be sad as a rule, but she could not stay inside one minute more, or she would burst into tears.

~

THE BINGLEY'S ride back from the Longbourn visit was filled with Miss Bingley and Mrs. Hurst's conversation regarding the Bennets and the shocking pronouncement by Mr. Collins. They hoped their brother would quit Netherfield soon so they would not be forced to be around Mr. Collins. The Bennet's lack of connections and low relations were now shown to be even worse than before with Mr. Collins now a permanent fixture.

Mr. Bingley was much unlike himself as he stared into the distance, having not joined in the conversation. He would have censured his sisters to be not so judgmental to a family that was in mourning, but Mr. Bingley was worried that if he did open his mouth, he would reveal his thoughts. Thoughts he knew his sisters were completely against. Therefore, he kept his confidences to himself.

Back at Netherfield there was one person Mr. Bingley was going to share his thoughts with, no matter how much that man did not want to hear anything about the Bennets.

CHAPTER 11

Mr. Bingley bounded up the steps of Netherfield. He took off his hat, coat, and gloves with as much speed as possible, handed them to his valet, and went in search of his friend, Mr. Darcy. Netherfield Park was a nice-sized house, but Mr. Bingley knew his friend's haunts. Mr. Bingley found him in the library in his favorite reading spot. His quick and loud footsteps alerted Mr. Darcy to his friend's heightened state.

"My God, man, what is wrong?" Mr. Darcy marked his book and set it down.

"Fitzwilliam, I have to do something! I cannot leave Miss Bennet there. She is so sad and morose. I do not want to speak ill of a parson, but their cousin, Mr.

Collins is an unreasonable man!" Mr. Bingley paced. "He does mean to marry one of the Bennet sisters and live at Longbourn. I cannot leave Miss Bennet to that fate."

"Are you sure that Mr. Collins has indeed chosen Miss Bennet to be his intended?"

Mr. Bingley stopped his pacing to face Mr. Darcy. "I have not. But she is obviously the best choice. She is the eldest, the most beautiful, all kindness and sweet-tempered. You even said Miss Bennet was the most handsome at the Meryton Assembly."

Mr. Darcy remembered he had said that, and at the time it had been true. However, he was not going to let himself think of a pair of fine eyes, a quick wit, and a lively personality and he no longer thought Miss Bennet was the most handsome. A connection, a marriage with that family could not happen. "So you mean to offer your hand to Miss Bennet though you do not know whether she is in any danger of being engaged to this Mr. Collins? Do you think that is a reasonable course of action?"

Mr. Bingley clenched his fists. "How can you be so calm, Fitzwilliam? Are you not concerned about

Miss Elizabeth? She could very well be chosen by Mr. Collins and forced to marry him."

Mr. Darcy straightened in his chair. "We have no proof that Mr. Collins will indeed throw them out if one does not marry him. That is gossip from Miss Bingley's maid. You heard nothing of it while you were at Longbourn?"

"It is not as if I could broach the subject while we were there."

"Well, you spoke about Mr. Collins marrying one of the Bennet girls."

"Oh, come now, Fitzwilliam. You know we could not ask Mr. Collins if he intended to throw out the entire Bennet family if one girl refused to marry him."

Mr. Darcy was distracted by the Bingley sisters walking towards them. "Are you working yourself up, Charles? We followed your loud voice all the way to the library."

"I am not working myself into a state, Caroline. Do not tell me you have no feelings for the Bennets. Their father was just buried and that cousin forcing one of them to marry him? It should not be legal. It has to be some... some sort of... extortion!"

"Charles, calm yourself down man," said Mr. Darcy. "Mr. Collins inherited Longbourn through an entailment. The estate is his now do to as he wishes. I heard nothing of the Bennets being forced to marry him. Just Mr. Collins wishing to do so."

"Can you not see that he will choose Miss Bennet?"

"I see nothing of the sort. From my limited contact, Miss Mary seems the best choice for him." Mr. Darcy picked up his book again, secure in the knowledge that a certain Bennet daughter was not in any danger.

"Tell me Fitzwilliam, that you are not the slightest bit concerned about Miss Elizabeth. She could very well be the one that Mr. Collins intends to marry. How would you feel if she was married to that man?"

Miss Bingley did not like the turn the discussion had taken. "I do not think that there is anything to worry about with the Bennets. Their father knew the estate was entailed and saved money for this very purpose. They will move and leave Longbourn to Mr. Collins. This is all a ridiculous rumor or ruse to force... Yes, that must be it." Miss Bingley turned to her brother. "It is a rumor they started to scare you into offering for Miss Bennet."

Mrs. Hurst nodded. "I believe you are right, Caroline. I can see Mrs. Bennet doing exactly that. She even mentioned at our ball that she expected Miss Bennet to be engaged soon to you, Charles. Surely she would not let the death of her husband get in her way."

Caroline turned to her sister. "So you see it too, Louisa? It makes perfect sense, does it not?"

Mr. Bingley frowned at his sisters. "I do not think this is a ruse at all. How could Mrs. Bennet have made this a ruse when I heard it from Mr. Collins himself? We all did. He intends to marry one of them."

Mr. Darcy observed his friend. "Would you really want to marry into the Bennet family? Do you remember how they behaved at your ball---the lack of propriety and decorum? Even Mr. Collins made a spectacle of himself. You really wish to be associated with that?"

"Please, Charles, think of us as well." Caroline wrapped her arm around Mr. Bingley's. "I do not want to have those younger Bennet girls as sisters, nor Mrs. Bennet as a relation." Caroline shared a look with her sister.

Mr. Bingley frowned and did not look with favor upon his sisters and friend at that moment. He had gotten the impression that things were not as they seemed at Longbourn. The family was much too morose and sad. Even his lovely Miss Bennet could not sit tall or even smile. Sadness over the death of a parent was to be expected, but... things did not seem right.

He also did not trust Mr. Darcy's opinion in this matter. He normally considered Mr. Darcy the most intelligent man he knew, and he still did, yet he was so sure of his intuition that he chose to not say any more until he had more information.

Mr. Darcy opened his book and read as the Bingley siblings talked amongst themselves. Mr. Darcy was used to these flights of emotion by his friend. Mr. Bingley often became worked up about things, but would come to reason the next day. Mr. Darcy was sure that was the case here.

CHAPTER 12

Several days of rain forced Elizabeth to go without her walks outside. It unfortunately left her open to being followed all over Longbourn by Mr. Collins. To escape him, she would spend time in her bedchamber or Mrs. Bennet's. She had a feeling that she knew whom he expected to marry him, but Elizabeth decided upon a course of action to circumvent that possibility.

"Mama, I have an idea regarding our difficult problem." Elizabeth sat in a chair next to her mother, who laid on the chaise.

"Oh, do not talk to me about that man! I cannot stand to hear his name. He will throw us all out in the streets. We will all die!" Mrs. Bennet covered her eyes with her arm to block out any light from further strengthening her headache.

"Mama! Please, I have come up with an idea that will work in our favor. Mr. Collins plans to marry one of us, however it does not stand to reason that he has to make the choice. We shall present to him which one of us he is to marry. We need only determine which one of us would be willing to marry Mr. Collins, so that the rest of us may have a place to live."

Mrs. Bennet put down her arm. "Oh, that is a good idea, Elizabeth. Oh yes, that would leave Jane available for Mr. Bingley. We cannot have Mr. Collins marrying Jane. Ring Hill to bring your sisters here at once!"

Elizabeth rang for Hill and soon all the Bennet girls were situated in Mrs. Bennet's bedchamber. Mrs. Bennet looked livelier than she had in weeks.

"Girls, girls, now I have had a thought about the situation we find ourselves in," Mrs. Bennet said as Elizabeth shared a small smile with Jane. "Instead of waiting for him to choose one of you, why do we not choose one of you first? One of you girls has to consider Mr. Collins somebody that they could live with, perhaps even admire." Mrs. Bennet ended her speech and looked directly at Mary. "Someone that perhaps shares in Mr. Collins' interests of sermons and music."

"Yes, Mary!" Lydia got up and leaned over to Mary. "Do marry him so that we do not have to! Then we will not be thrown out of our home. I do not want to leave Longbourn and all the officers in Meryton!"

"Me neither!" Kitty leaned forward and also implored Mary to save them.

Mary stood from where she had sat on the edge of Mrs. Bennet's bed. "I do not find the idea distasteful, though I do not like the idea that one of us is to be presented as a sacrifice for the others. Marriage is a very holy union in the eyes of God and should not be looked on or approached in this manner. We should let Mr. Collins make his choice as is proper and right."

Mrs. Bennet scoffed. "Mary, we are in a difficult situation. Mr. Collins stated that he will marry one of you or we are all to be gone with even less time now! It is your duty to marry Mr. Collins since you have the most similar interests and you have admired him before." Mrs. Bennet rose from her chaise. "It is all settled. We will go once and inform Mr. Collins."

Lydia and Kitty scampered out of the room, followed by Mrs. Bennet, who was in a much cheerier mood now that she had a solution to the problem of Mr. Collins. Elizabeth and Jane shared another smile, glad that it had been easy to convince Mrs. Bennet of their idea. Other than giving them a place to live, the idea had the added benefit of saving them from having to marry Mr. Collins.

And so, to the main floor they all went in high spirits that came with the knowledge that their most pressing problem was solved and all would soon be right again. Of course, they would have to deal with Mary as the mistress of the house, and she did have a tendency to be overbearing, but surely that would not be that bad as being employed for a living.

They found Mr. Collins in the drawing room as he stood in front of the fireplace having been practicing a sermon before the entire Bennet family entered the room. "Oh, my. How kind of you to come and be an audience for my latest sermon. I wrote it for the new curate to use. I am preparing many sermons as examples of the kind that I have given before to the parishioners of Hunsford so that the curate may know what they and I expect for their guidance."

"Mr. Collins, I think you shall be quite happy with the news we have to share with you." Mrs. Bennet smiled at Mr. Collins as if she had not glared at him for the at least the last sennight.

"News to share?" Mr. Collins looked at all the Bennets, but though their countenances were not the morose sadness he had grown used to, they were also not filled with joy.

"Yes Mr. Collins. We have decided which of the girls will be your bride. Come forward, Mary."

Mary walked forward and smiled at Mr. Collins. She would be mistress of Longbourn and tell her sisters what to do. She was excited at the prospect of curbing their reading of novels and running to Meryton to chase after the officers. Mary was also gratified that she would not end up a spinster living with her mother in a relative's house at their mercy.

Mr. Collins was surprised but quickly recovered and gave a small bow to Mary. "I am quite appreciative of your kind and thoughtful offer. I cannot be remiss by mentioning the flattery and honor you do me by presenting yourself to be my wife. It shows a good heart, but I fear you have misjudged the situation. It is I who will choose who will be blessed by being my wife." Mary's countenance changed dramatically, but Mr. Collins continued. "Now is a good time as any to announce that I ask Elizabeth Bennet to be my wife." Mr. Collins bowed in Elizabeth's direction and thereby missed the horror that showed on so many of the Bennet countenances.

The pandemonium that statement elicited was instantaneous. Mary fled the room while Mrs. Bennet sat down, knowing the headstrong nature of her second-eldest daughter. If they were to depend upon Elizabeth to marry Mr. Collins, they were all doomed indeed.

Elizabeth could not look away from Mr. Collins. She saw his sweaty face, crooked smile, and arm outstretched to help her rise from her chair. "No." Elizabeth stood. "No, Mr. Collins, I am sorry, but I am unable to accept."

"Elizabeth! You cannot say no. You have to marry Mr. Collins!" Mrs. Bennet had recovered and stood now in front of Elizabeth having pushed aside Mr. Collins in her rush to correct her obstinate daughter.

Lydia also would not stay in her seat. "We shall be turned out of our house on the streets. Do not be so selfish!" Lydia ran around to stand right next to Mrs. Bennet.

Mr. Collins did not seem negatively affected by Elizabeth's answer. "I understand, my dear cousin, that this may be a surprise to you, but I have long admired your kindness, wit, and intelligence. I shall give you time to become acquainted with the idea, but I would like to marry quickly as I need to return to Hunsford in a fortnight to guide the new curate."

Elizabeth ignored all others and focused on Mr. Collins. "Mr. Collins, I do not believe you understand me. I shall not be marrying you at all."

Mrs. Bennet screeched in response. "You cannot do this to us, Elizabeth Bennet! I shall not be turned out on the streets because you will not do your duty. Go to your room! You shall not leave it until you give a favorable answer!"

"Mama!" said Jane. "You cannot do this to Lizzy! It is not right to lock her in our room."

"It is not right that she wants to throw her entire family out into the streets, either!" Mrs. Bennet would not change her mind.

Elizabeth turned and walked upstairs into her bedchamber and closed the door. She did not have much time to herself because she had been followed upstairs by all her family except Mary.

"You cannot do this, Lizzy!" Lydia flew at her from the doorway. "I do not want to have to work. I am not even ten and six! I have balls and parties and officers to be with. I will not let you throw me out of my home and Meryton where I have all of my friends and acquaintances!"

"Indeed, she cannot, Lydia." Mrs. Bennet came right up to Elizabeth. "You have to do this, Elizabeth. We all know one of you girls must marry him and it was your idea to select one of you. Well, now it is you he selected, Elizabeth. You must do your duty to save us all from ruin."

Elizabeth stood at the window and looked out on the grounds without seeing them. She knew that she had become a favorite in Mr. Collins' eyes, but she did not think he would offer for her as Mary was the most obvious choice. Now, he had offered for her and she was in shock and knew not what to do about the situation.

How easy it was to offer up a sister instead of herself. But now that she was to be the sacrifice, to be married to Mr. Collins to save them from being thrown out, she did not want to do it at all. She could not imagine, for one moment, being married to that man, to live with him for the rest of her life, to even have children with him.

Elizabeth turned to face her family. "I cannot do it. I cannot marry him and have children with him. I cannot. I love you all and I would not have you thrown out. There must be something else we can do."

"Mama," said Jane, "you know locking Lizzy in our room is not going to save us. There has to be something else, some other way."

"Thank you, Jane." Elizabeth was glad to have Jane on her side. She knew though that if they left Longbourn and moved away, Mr. Bingley would forever be out of Jane's reach. Elizabeth did not wish that for her at all. But she also could not bear to sacrifice herself to Mr. Collins. "I must go. I need to take a walk---"

"You are not allowed to leave this room, Elizabeth. You will stay in here until you give a favorable answer to Mr. Collins." Mrs. Bennet stormed out of the room followed by Lydia and Kitty.

Elizabeth turned to Jane who gave her a little smile and opened her arms. Elizabeth rushed into them and hugged her dear sister. "Oh Jane, what shall we do? What will become of us?"

CHAPTER 13

Elizabeth did not leave her room. Every time she opened the door to sneak out, someone yelled at her. Elizabeth had never had her entire family, except Jane, unhappy with her. Mary did not harass her to marry Mr. Collins, but she was upset that Mr. Collins had turned her aside in favor of Elizabeth.

Hill brought her food, and she did have a book to read, though she could not concentrate well enough to read much. Elizabeth wrote to her friend Charlotte Lucas, but Mrs. Bennet forbade the letter to be sent to Lucas Lodge. Elizabeth was sure that if the Gardiners had still been at Meryton, they would have never allowed this treatment of her to continue.

However, they were back in London and Elizabeth was not allowed to send a letter to them.

She therefore had nothing to do except sit and think, which was exactly what her mother had intended. That did not mean her sisters did not visit her, though. Jane spent as much time with her as she could before Mrs. Bennet yelled at her to leave Lizzy alone. She also snuck in flowers and books. Lydia came into her room with Kitty quite often, not to bolster Elizabeth's spirits but to inform her of how cruel and selfish she was. Elizabeth wished she could fit under the bed to hide from them. She was not a coward or a weak person, but she could not deal with this constant pressure.

How horrible was Mr. Collins to force marriage upon one of them or they would all be turned out and destitute? Elizabeth thought of the situation from many paths but could not find a solution other than for Mr. Bingley to offer for Jane and the entire family move to Netherfield Hall. However, that solution was impossible as none of them could leave Longbourn as they were in mourning, and Jane could not write an unmarried man.

While she sat at the window, Elizabeth had the misfortune to see her Aunt Phillips approach Longbourn. She groaned and hid her head in her hands. Once Aunt Phillips left Longbourn, news of Elizabeth being locked in her room would be all over Meryton. She thought of George Wickham and how mortified she would be for him to know she was locked in her room like a child. The last time she had seen him was when he paid his condolences with the other officers. She could not imagine an amiable man like him would stay unattached for long.

Elizabeth heard her mother's loud voice as she lamented her ungrateful daughter that would have them all thrown out to live on the streets. Her wailing wore upon Elizabeth's mood. It was hard to stay upbeat when you were the subject of continual degradation by your own family.

She managed to last two days locked in her room before she could not stay one more minute. She heard Hill move about downstairs as the light of a new day lit her bedchamber. Elizabeth dressed quickly, verified Jane was still asleep, opened the door, and crept downstairs, where she put on her boots and snuck out the front door. Finally, she was free.

She had walked in her bedchamber as much as possible the last few days, but that was nothing compared to a walk outside. She walked until her legs had stretched, and then she ran, pumped her arms, breathed in the crisp air, and felt the cool air against her cheeks. She walked up the hill of Oakham Mount to her favorite place, a large rock at the top of the hill where she liked to sit and look upon the countryside.

Elizabeth stood and gazed upon Meryton, Lucas Lodge, the Longs' house, and even Netherfield Hall. If only there were some way she could get word to Mr. Bingley that he needed to marry Jane to save them all... but she knew she could never do that as it would be far outside the bounds of propriety. Plus, she was not sure any man would do what he was told, especially when it came to offering for someone. Even though Elizabeth was sure Mr. Bingley would offer for Jane at some point, she did not know how to force that to happen quickly.

Elizabeth finally sat upon the large rock as her spirits dropped. There really was no outcome for her situation other than to marry Mr. Collins. She shuddered as she seriously considered being Mr. Collins' wife. To deal with his stupidity, self-importance, and sermon-reading. Elizabeth wiped at the tears that ran down her face. She could not bear it.

Elizabeth remembered Mr. Bennet when he told her that she was the type of person that would not be happy if she married a man she did not respect. Mr. Collins was the epitome of a man she did not respect. Would she have to be shackled to this man to save her family? Elizabeth's emotions overcame her, and she cried.

~

Mr. Darcy loved nothing more than to ride across the countryside in the early sunlight. The new day's light turned everything into a scene akin to a fairy-tale. Mr. Darcy guided Bucephalus up a narrow path on the hill. This was one of his favorite riding trails in the countryside around Netherfield. It led to a wondrous view of the countryside. Hertfordshire was not as beautiful as Derbyshire, but it was still a pleasant view.

The closer Mr. Darcy got to the top of the hill, the louder a discordant sound became. He could not make out the noise until nearly at the top of the hill when he realized it was the sound of someone desperately crying. Mr. Darcy slowed Bucephalus to a walk, careful to not frighten whoever was distraught. He spied a figure perched atop the very boulder Mr. Darcy liked to sit upon. He grew closer and realized it was a woman dressed in a bonnet and coat, not of the latest fashions or highest quality, but definitely a member of the gentry.

Mr. Darcy was embarrassed at intruding upon someone's distress. He felt he should offer help, yet perhaps the person did not wish to be disturbed? Why else would someone climb the hill but to be alone? Or perhaps the woman was injured and needed help. These inclinations warred with the instincts of preservation that Mr. Darcy's father had impressed upon him as a young lad. He was an eligible bachelor with land and money, therefore he was always cautious of being accidentally compromised. To be alone with an unattached woman of the gentry was to court disaster.

Mr. Darcy nudged his horse closer to determine who rested upon the large rock. The woman faced away from him, towards the best view of the countryside. For Mr. Darcy to see their face he would also be seen. He did not want to leave someone who was in need of assistance, but he also did not want a false story by an enterprising woman to trap him in marriage either. Mr. Darcy eyed the woman's figure but did not see evidence of an injury. The woman even moved her legs at one point, relieving him that she had hurt a leg.

Convinced there was no injury, Mr. Darcy realized the woman was most probably one of the Bennet daughters, mourning the loss of Mr. Bennet. Mr. Darcy knew how great a loss that could be, having lost both his parents. Mr. Darcy slowly backed Bucephalus away and turned him back down Oakham Mount. He would leave the woman alone in her mourning and continue his early morning ride elsewhere.

Mr. Darcy had a stray thought as he rode away, that the person crying might have been the Bennet girl marrying Mr. Collins. However, he decided that was foolish as Mr. Collins had not forced any of the Bennet girls to marry him. No, Mr. Collins would offer for one and it would be up to the girl to accept or refuse the offer. Mr. Darcy was sure that everything would continue to be fine at Longbourn notwithstanding Mr. Bingley's concerns.

Elizabeth stayed on Oakham Mount for some time. She knew if she refused Mr. Collins, they would all be turned out and most likely sooner than Mr. Collins' deadline. They would have to find a small house and the eldest three would need to find employment. That also made certain that Elizabeth and Jane would not make a good marriage, and Jane would never see Mr. Bingley again. Could she do that to her sister? Could she do that to all her sisters?

Elizabeth knew deep in her heart that she could not. But she also could not fathom being married to Mr. Collins, nor having children with him. Elizabeth shuddered and swallowed several times as she was nearly ill. There was no other way out of their present situation.

She stood and walked back down to Longbourn. She had prayed for a miracle, even before Mr. Collins had offered for her, but none had happened. Elizabeth realized her disappearance would have been noticed by now. Her family could continue to yell at her as much as they wanted, it did not matter.

Elizabeth opened the front door and walked up the stairs but was stopped by her mother's voice. "Elizabeth? Elizabeth, I told you to stay in your room! Where did you go?"

Elizabeth stopped on the second step and raised her eyes upwards. She turned around to face the entryway. "I walked, Mama. I went to Oakham Mount and thought of Papa."

Mrs. Bennet severe countenance lessened. She looked down, pursed her lips and then looked back up at Elizabeth. "That still did not give you the right to leave when you knew your punishment. Here is a letter from the Gardiners, and they included a note for you. I daresay it would be good for you to read."

Elizabeth raised her eyebrows as she held out her hand for the note. She had expected her mother to be in a panic at her whereabouts or least yell at her. Puzzled by this, Elizabeth read the short note.

"Dearest Lizzy,

I was sad to hear the news that Mr. Collins chose you to be his wife. I know this is not the match we would want for you, nor the kind of man you have mentioned that you hoped to marry. I ask you to think of your options and all permutations before you decide upon a course of action. Your decision will have far-reaching and long-lasting effects. I know you will make the best decision.

Love,

Aunt Madeline Gardiner"

Elizabeth could not breathe. Her legs collapsed, and she sat hard on the stairs. There was her guidance she had prayed for.

Elizabeth wiped her face, and as if from far away, she heard herself inform Mrs. Bennet that she would marry Mr. Collins.

CHAPTER 14

Mr. Collins walked in Longbourn and around Meryton, as proud as a peacock. He would marry one of the Bennet beauties, the second-eldest, Elizabeth. Mr. Collins had admired her from the beginning with her womanly figure. He could not wait for their wedding night. He had even told Elizabeth that they would be married by a license and not by having the Banns read in the parish like commoners.

Elizabeth had not much cared what happened after she told Mrs. Bennet she would marry Mr. Collins. Her life felt as if it was not her own anymore. It was scandalous that they were getting married during their mourning period for Mr. Bennet, however, Mr. Collins set the demand and she had to comply.

Aunt Phillips stopped by Longbourn with news that the real reason behind the fast marriage to Mr. Collins was out, that he had forced Elizabeth to marry him or the entire family would be out on the streets. Opinions of Mr. Collins were turning against him. That the intelligent and beautiful second-eldest to be forced to marry such a silly man as Mr. Collins had many feeling sad for Miss Elizabeth. However, condolences would do nothing to change the future that stretched out for decades before her. Elizabeth would soon be Mrs. Collins and subject to her husband's commands.

Elizabeth shuddered as she sat in her room and stared out the window. Her relationship with her entire family had changed since Mr. Collins had offered for her. She could understand the desperation that caused them to treat her the way they had. She had forgiven them, but she had not yet forgiven Mr. Bennet for putting her in this position.

Though the Banns were not read in church on Sunday, the entire town knew the wedding of Mr. Collins and Elizabeth Bennet would happen quickly due to his need to return to the Hunsford parsonage to give guidance to the new curate. The dressmaker came to Longbourn to measure Elizabeth and have her pick out the fabric for her wedding dress, which was just a simple new dress. Elizabeth left that decision to Mrs. Bennet and her sisters as she could not summon any interest.

~

Mr. Bingley paced in the sitting room as his sisters, Mr. Hurst, and Mr. Darcy played whist. His continual pacing and stopping to look back at their table finally drove Caroline to speak. "Charles, do stop that. You are making it difficult for me to concentrate on my hand."

"I apologize Caroline," said Mr. Bingley, "but I cannot help but be concerned from what I have heard in Meryton this afternoon."

The entire table turned to look at Mr. Bingley, except Mr. Hearst who pointed to his glass and asked a servant for a refill.

"What news from Meryton?" said Louisa.

Mr. Bingley walked closer to their card table. "It is quite upsetting, and I would not believe it myself if I had not heard everyone in town talking about it." Mr. Bingley looked at Mr. Darcy with apprehension.

Mr. Darcy raised an eyebrow. "Well do tell us then, Charles. Do not keep us in suspense."

"You might not want to hear this, Fitzwilliam."

"The only news I do not want to hear is about the Bennet family."

Mr. Bingley flattened his lips and continued to stare at his friend. "I feel this is news you should hear."

Mr. Darcy stood. "I must excuse myself then." He bowed and walked away.

Mr. Bingley followed. "Come now, Darcy, you are being silly. This is news that you need to hear."

"I do not care to hear a word about the Bennet family, you know that, Charles. Nothing you say would make a bit of difference in my life." Mr. Darcy walked out of the room.

Mr. Bingley stood at the empty doorway. He wanted to knock sense into his friend's head for being so obstinate and stupid.

"Charles, leave Fitzwilliam alone. We are interested in any news regarding the Bennet family, are we not Louisa?" Caroline turned to her sister with a smile.

"We are indeed. Charles, we will listen to the latest gossip about the poor Bennet family." The sisters giggled.

Mr. Bingley turned and stormed to the card table. "You would not believe the news! I cannot believe it myself, but I have heard it from many sources." Mr. Bingley hesitated, having realized the news might, no, most definitely would garner the wrong reaction from his sisters.

"Come on, Charles." Louisa shared a confused look with her sister at the reticence their brother displayed.

"Mr. Collins is going to marry Miss Elizabeth Bennet." Shock showed plainly upon the countenances of the Bingley sisters, but one of them smiled quickly.

"Indeed? Shocking. I would have thought the one that played the pianoforte so badly at our ball would marry Mr. Collins. What was her name?" Caroline turned to her sister.

"Mary, that was her name."

"This is not an amusing account, sisters. Mr. Collins is forcing her to marry him or he will throw the entire family out of their home!"

That got their attention. "Throw them out? Really? Is not Mr. Collins a parson?"

Mr. Bingley nodded. "Yes, he is. Not only that but he is a parson of a village next to where Mr. Darcy's aunt lives. His aunt recommended Mr. Collins for the position! I am aghast at this news! For a parson, a man of the church, to act in such a manner to a family that has recently lost their father. It is insupportable!"

Caroline and Louisa shared a look again, as it was not common to see their brother agitated over something that did not affect him. "How does this affect you, Charles?" Caroline asked her brother. "I admit I am surprised to see you so bothered by this."

"Because this is not right. It is wrong for someone to treat the Bennets in this way, especially a relation of theirs. I do not know what to do about the situation, though. Especially since Mr. Darcy does not seem concerned in the slightest about Miss Elizabeth's fate."

Caroline did not like to hear Mr. Darcy's and Elizabeth Bennet's name together. "What makes you think Mr. Darcy would be concerned about Miss Elizabeth Bennet? I have heard him say that the only tolerable one was the eldest."

Mr. Bingley flattened his lips as he stared at his sister Caroline. He knew she had been angling for Mr. Darcy ever since they had become friends. Mr. Bingley did not want to cause strife with his thoughts on the subject. He also was not going to share that Mr. Darcy held Miss Elizabeth in high regard. "I thought Mr. Darcy would want to be notified as he is a charitable man and does much for those in need. I am frustrated that I cannot even talk to him about the situation."

Caroline narrowed her eyes. "Then you best leave it alone. The Bennets do not have any situation now with Miss Elizabeth Bennet marrying Mr. Collins. He will not throw them out at all if that was ever the case." Caroline turned back towards the table. "It is your hand to deal, Mr. Hurst."

Mr. Bingley stared at Caroline and Louisa frustrated beyond measure. He knew that once his friend Mr. Darcy set his mind to a course, he never veered from it. But he also thought Mr. Darcy was being uncommonly stupid.

Mr. Bingley knew Mr. Darcy cared for Elizabeth, as his eyes were often on her whenever they were in the same room. No matter what Mr. Darcy thought of their lack of connections and behavior, Mr. Bingley would not let that stop him from offering for the eldest Bennet daughter as soon as their mourning period was over. He was sure Mr. Darcy would regret it if Elizabeth Bennet married Mr. Collins. But Mr. Bingley did not know how to bring it up to him.

CHAPTER 15

The wedding of Mr. Collins and Elizabeth Bennet would take place that Saturday morning. The wedding breakfast would be held at Longbourn, and then Mr. and Mrs. Collins would set off directly to Hunsford and spend their wedding night in the parsonage.

The entire Bennet family were relieved, and Mr. Collins was back in Mrs. Bennet's good graces. She told her sister Mrs. Phillips that they were lucky that Mr. Collins would allow them to stay at Longbourn.

Other than Elizabeth, only Mary was unhappy with the upcoming wedding. She had admired Mr. Collins since he first came to Longbourn and was quite put out with how easily he deflected her offer and chose Elizabeth. She knew Elizabeth was marrying Mr. Collins only out of duty, which stung even more for Mary. It would not have been a duty for her. However, she tried her best to avoid the wedding preparations and hoped she could leave Longbourn soon as it would not be pleasant to live in the same house with the man she had hoped to marry.

Elizabeth would have found it humorous, if she felt remotely like laughing, that when she was forced to stay in her room she wanted to be out of it, but now that she could go anywhere, she wanted to stay in her room. She loathed to be among the rest of the family, who were happy that everything was resolved in their favor. Elizabeth was the sacrificial goat on the altar of Mr. Collins' hubris. She could not imagine what her life would be like married to him. But soon she would know as it was Thursday, and the wedding was to take place on Saturday.

Mr. Bingley approached Mr. Darcy in the game room and waited to speak until after Fitzwilliam had pocketed a shot. "I am going to London tomorrow on a quick errand. Would you like to accompany me?"

Mr. Darcy stood. "A quick errand? Would you stay the night or return the same day?"

"Oh, I would spend at least a night or two for sure. It is not an urgent errand and I am quite sure that I will need to run a few errands for Caroline when she hears I am going to London."

Mr. Darcy shrugged. "Yes, I will accompany you."

Mr. Bingley smiled and nodded. "Perfect. I shall direct my valet to pack a small case." Mr. Bingley left the room, leaving a curious Mr. Darcy behind.

~

THE BINGLEY CARRIAGE left early in the morning Friday with Mr. Bingley and Mr. Darcy. Mr. Bingley was correct in that he did have a few errands to run for both of his sisters. The men chose not to ride their horses, no matter how much Mr. Darcy loved to ride his beloved Bucephalus, because of the weather and the amount of packages Mr. Bingley would bring back due to his sister's errands. Mr. Bingley was uncommonly chatty and anxious on the ride towards London.

"Charles, I have never seen you this anxious. What awaits you in London?"

Mr. Bingley smiled and shrugged. "I am just nervous. I feel we are going to have a storm soon and I want to make sure we return before it strikes."

Mr. Darcy frowned and looked out the carriage window. "How can you know we are going to have a storm?"

"Oh, something one of the farmers in the village said. You know how they can determine the weather with their strange methods such as brown caterpillars and such. I heard one state that a bad storm was coming."

Now, Mr. Darcy was quite suspicious of Mr. Bingley. "But, are we not planning to stay in London for a few nights? Will we not bypass the storm?"

Mr. Bingley reddened. "Oh, yes. Yes, quite." And then he looked out the carriage window.

Mr. Darcy continued to stare at Mr. Bingley and ran through possibilities in his mind of what his friend was about and why he wanted to return to Meryton, even though he told Darcy they would be staying a few nights in London. Mr. Darcy could not figure it out.

~

THEIR CARRIAGE PULLED into one of the many inns on the road to London. The gentlemen climbed out as the horses were changed for fresh ones. The men went into the inn and were seated in the common room. Though they were men of quality, there was no available separate room for them to use.

They settled in for a quick bite of tea and scones when Mr. Bingley brought up the subject that had been in his thoughts all morning. "I am quite surprised that you are so calm, Fitzwilliam, and agreed to go on this trip to London with me."

Mr. Darcy slathered marmalade on his scone. "Oh, and why is that?"

"Why, the wedding of Mr. Collins is taking place tomorrow in Meryton." Mr. Bingley stared at Mr. Darcy.

"And why would that concern me in the slightest? I find Mr. Collins an incomprehensible boar."

"Because he is marrying one of the Bennet girls. Are you not interested as to who he is marrying?"

Mr. Darcy continued to look down. "Not in the slightest. He is probably marrying that quiet one that is not one of the eldest sisters. The one who cannot sing nor play the pianoforte with any reasonable skill." Mr. Darcy's thoughts were on the second-eldest Bennet girl, Elizabeth. Her large brown eyes, impertinent mouth, shapely figure, and quick intelligent mind.

"And that is why I am so surprised you are traveling today and do not display any concern at all."

Mr. Darcy realized Mr. Bingley had been speaking to him, but he had completely missed it. "What was that again? I apologize, I was distracted."

Mr. Bingley leaned forward. "I said Mr. Collins is marrying Miss Elizabeth Bennet tomorrow in Meryton."

"What?!" Mr. Darcy's exclamation was so loud that the rest of the patrons at the inn stared in his direction. "You cannot be serious? Miss Elizabeth Bennet to marry Mr. Collins?"

Mr. Bingley nodded. "It is true, and it is taking place tomorrow morning."

Mr. Darcy stood so quickly that his chair fell backwards with a thud.

Mr. Bingley was shocked, as his friend normally displayed perfect gentlemen-like manners wherever he went.

"Are you certain? I cannot believe she would do such a thing."

"I was in Meryton myself yesterday and heard the news spoken everywhere. Mr. Collins was going to throw the entire family out unless one of them married him and he chose Elizabeth. She is sacrificing herself to save her family, Fitzwilliam." Mr. Bingley stood and hoped his friend was shocked enough to do something.

"We must leave at once! We have to return to Meryton. No, we have to go to London!" Darcy stormed towards the door and then turned back to the table. "Come, Charles, we have no time to spare! We need to go to London and then back to Meryton with all haste!" Mr. Darcy threw coins on the table, then grabbed his friend's arm and walked quickly out of the inn.

~

Mr. Darcy's behavior was much different during the rest of the trip to London. Now, it was Mr. Bingley who was calm, while Mr. Darcy was so anxious he could barely sit. "Can these horses not go any faster? Did I not tell the driver to make them go as fast as they possibly could?"

Mr. Bingley smiled at his friend.

"Do not sit there and smile at me so smugly, Charles. We need to get to London immediately!"

"Darcy, I believe you told the driver not ten minutes ago to go faster. I do not think they can go any faster than they currently are." Mr. Bingley continued to smile though Mr. Darcy frowned at him.

"Why are you smiling at me, Charles? I thought you were my friend."

"I am. As a matter of fact, I am your best friend, because are we not on our way to London to purchase a special license? You after being told the woman you admire is getting married tomorrow?"

"I fail to see how that makes you my best friend when I just now found that out!"

"Was it not you, Fitzwilliam, who stated that you did not want to hear anything at all about the Bennet family? How else could I have told you that Elizabeth Bennet was getting married to Mr. Collins except to come up with an excuse to go to London and have you in the carriage with me?"

Mr. Darcy sat back in his seat and smiled at his best friend. "I thank you, Charles. You are a sly one, are you not?"

"I thought I was going to go mad with your stubborn obstinacy. I had to think of some way to tell you in which you could not storm out of the room, which was your usual habit."

Mr. Darcy bowed to Mr. Bingley. "I acknowledge a superior schemer. If this all resolves itself satisfactorily, I will owe all my happiness to you."

"I do not see how it could not end satisfactorily. It is still early in the morning and she is not getting married until tomorrow morning. We have more than enough time to make things end happily."

Both friends smiled at each other as the first snowflake began to fall outside.

"I know you have admired Miss Elizabeth for months now, but do you know if she feels the same in return?"

Mr. Darcy frowned at his friend. "At this point I do not think it matters. I will not let her marry that buffoon to save her family. He is most decidedly beneath her."

Mr. Bingley smiled even wider. "Then you must have no objections to my offering for the eldest Bennet then? Since you are marrying the second-eldest?"

Mr. Darcy closed his eyes, smiled and then laughed. He opened his eyes and nodded at Mr. Bingley. "Well done, Charles. Well done, indeed. You have me in checkmate. No, I have no objections at all. And I think you would be doing Miss Bennet a great honor by asking her to marry you."

Having reached the Doctors Commons in London, both men applied for and purchased their special licenses from the Archbishop of Canterbury. Now they could marry their intendeds anywhere and at any time. Neither of them could stop smiling. However, those smiles took a decidedly downward turn as they walked to the carriage and realized that snow was falling quite rapidly.

"Where did this come from? I do not recall this much snow when we arrived in London."

Mr. Darcy turned to his friend. "Did you not say in the carriage that you heard a big storm was coming?"

Mr. Bingley turned a shade of vermillion. "Actually, I made it all up. I had to think of some reason to fool you as to why I was so nervous. I could not tell you the truth that I had brought you along under false pretenses."

Both men trudged to the carriage as they worried over whether they could even make it back to Meryton tonight. "Driver, carry on back to Meryton as quick as you can!" Mr. Bingley said.

CHAPTER 16

The day of Elizabeth's wedding arrived with a sparkling winter landscape, the aftermath of the winter storm. Glistening snow was everywhere, turning the countryside into a wonderland.

Mrs. Bennet opened the door to Elizabeth's bedchamber. "Elizabeth, look outside. It is a gorgeous day for your wedding---such glistening and sparkling. I have never seen a more perfect day."

She opened the curtains to let in the sun. "It would have been impossible to have a more beautiful day for a winter wedding. You are a lucky girl, Elizabeth." She turned to see her second-eldest daughter put the pillow over her head.

She walked over to the bed and pulled the pillow, but it would not budge. "Elizabeth, get up. Today is your wedding day, and we have to get you ready. Hill will bring your hot bath shortly." Mrs. Bennet walked out and closed the door.

Elizabeth was surprised that she had managed to fall asleep at some point during the night. She shuddered, not from cold but from the horror of what lay ahead of her. The wedding, she could handle. It was the kiss and... what came after that... she could not. Tears rolled out of her eyes.

The bedchamber door burst open with her younger sisters. "Lizzy! Lizzy, get up! Today is the day you marry Mr. Collins and save us all!" Kitty and Lydia joined hands and swung in a circle with laughter.

"Have you not even looked at your wedding dress yet? It is very fine." Kitty took the lid off the box and admired the plain yet pretty gown.

Mrs. Bennet returned to the room followed by Hill and Beth, a maid. "Girls, get away from the dress. We must keep it looking good for the wedding. Now put the tub there and fill it up." Mrs. Bennet directed the servants as they carried in the hot water. She approached the bed again.

"Get up. You are not a child, so do not act like one."

Mrs. Bennet turned towards the door. "Girls, leave the dress alone! Elizabeth needs to get ready for her wedding."

The servants filled the tub with hot water and then closed the door. Elizabeth was all alone with her thoughts again. She did not want to bathe in rose oil for Mr. Collins. She did not want to put on the wedding dress. Tears rolled down her face, but she still had not thought of a way out of the situation that would not leave her family destitute. She slowly crawled out of bed to face the day.

"Mr. Collins, do not go upstairs. It is bad luck for you to see the bride before the wedding!"

A knock at the door followed that shout. "My dearest Elizabeth, I cannot wait until you are my wife. I am leaving now for the church and I will see you soon, my dearest."

Elizabeth swallowed rapidly to keep herself from getting sick. She did not know how she could get through the wedding if she could not even handle hearing Mr. Collins' voice.

The door opened and Jane walked in. "Lizzy, how are you faring?"

Elizabeth looked up at her sister. "I am to marry Mr. Collins today. That is all that needs to be said."

"I am so sorry, Lizzy. I wish you would not have to go through with this."

Elizabeth looked up at her sister and smiled. "Thank you."

"You are not wearing the wedding dress?"

"I do not feel like wearing it. It would be inappropriate for me to wear that when I am in mourning for Papa."

"I am truly sorry, Lizzy. I fear I do not know what I would have done if Mr. Collins had chosen me."

"If he had chosen you, I would have forced him to choose another. You are destined for your Mr. Bingley."

Jane sat next to Elizabeth on the bed. "I still wish the same for you, Lizzy. I do not want to believe that this is your fate. I have prayed much for another resolution."

Elizabeth squeezed her sister's hand. "I fear we are out of time now, Jane."

Mrs. Bennet called from downstairs. "Girls! Elizabeth, we need to leave now! They are all waiting for us."

Elizabeth shuddered. Jane squeezed her hand and stood. Elizabeth wrapped her arms around herself and hunched forward. "I cannot do it, Jane. I cannot. I think of leaving to go to church and I am ill."

Elizabeth heard the front door open and close, then the sounds of Lydia and Kitty climbing in the carriage. They were chattering and happy. Loud footsteps came up the stairs and approached the bedchamber.

"What is taking so long? You are going to be late for your own wedding! You can not do that, the villagers will talk. Come down now, Elizabeth." Mrs. Bennet was dressed in her fine coat and hat. She pulled at Elizabeth's arm. "Jane, go downstairs and get in the carriage."

Jane left, and Elizabeth still could not make herself move.

"Elizabeth, get in the carriage this instant! I will have the servants carry you out if I have to!"

"I cannot, Mama. Please, I cannot go through with this. You know how unsuitable a match this is."

"Elizabeth Bennet, I have never heard a more selfish and uncaring plea. The fate of this entire family rests on you. This is no time for dramatics! You must get into the carriage!"

Elizabeth did not move.

"I will send for your uncle, Mr. Gardiner. He will get you out of your room and into the church."

Mrs. Bennet and the rest of the Bennet family climbed into their carriage and set off for the church in Meryton. Elizabeth was glad for the delay. It felt like a reprieve, though she knew the outcome would still be the same.

CHAPTER 17

The Bennet carriage pulled up in front of the church. The entire Bennet family, except Elizabeth, climbed out. Mr. Gardiner had waited outside the church as he was to escort his niece up the aisle.

Mrs. Bennet was thankful that he was outside the church. "Brother, you have to go back and bring Lizzy here. She will not leave! My nerves are fluttering and we are going to be thrown out if she does not marry Mr. Collins!"

Mr. Gardiner was not surprised by this. Elizabeth was the brightest and most lively of all the Bennet girls, and he could not imagine it would be easy for her to marry someone so unlike her. "Do not fear, sister. I will bring her here. Go in the church now and I will return with her."

Mr. Gardiner was about to climb into the waiting carriage when he stopped to stare. A carriage covered in snow approached the church. It must have traveled through the snowstorm the night before. Who would have come from out of town for this wedding?

Mr. Gardiner approached the carriage as the door opened and he saw a person wrapped in blankets. "Do you need assistance?"

"Has the wedding of Mr. Collins and Miss Elizabeth Bennet taken place yet?"

"No. As a matter of fact, I am on my way to bring the bride." Mr. Gardiner was now quite curious.

"Please do not, sir." Mr. Gardiner straightened at this impertinence from this unknown man. "I implore you to bring the parson to Longbourn. Tell him that Miss Elizabeth needs to be persuaded."

"And what is the meaning of this, sir? Who are you?" said Mr. Gardiner.

"I am the man who is going to marry her instead. I am Mr. Fitzwilliam Darcy."

Mr. Gardiner stepped back in astonishment. He had heard of Mr. Darcy from Derbyshire from his wife who grew up in that county. Mr. Darcy was the richest man in the county, one of the wealthiest men in all of England. This could not possibly be the same man, though. How could he have heard of this wedding or Elizabeth for that matter?

"I have heard of a Mr. Darcy from Derbyshire but that is far north of here." Mr. Gardiner would ascertain the identity of this man before he left to get Elizabeth.

"I am Mr. Darcy from Derbyshire and have been staying with my friend Mr. Bingley at Netherfield Park." Mr. Bingley leaned forward. "I have admired your niece and have returned from London with a special license."

"You have cut this quite close, Mr. Darcy. Why did you wait until the day of her wedding to another man? I have never heard her mention you." Mr. Gardiner would not let his awe show, as his first duty was to his niece.

These were awkward questions for Mr. Darcy. He fidgeted, unused to having to answer for any of his decisions. "I only recently heard of the proposed wedding. We must make haste before someone comes out. You will do me a great favor if you could bring the parson to Longbourn."

Mr. Gardiner was aware that Mr. Darcy did not answer the question of why his niece had never mentioned this Mr. Darcy. Mrs. Bennet had not either. If there was a man as fine as Mr. Darcy interested in one of her girls, Mrs. Bennet would not tire of speaking of it.

"Forgive me, but this is quite extraordinary. How can I be assured that you are who you say? If you have heard of the wedding, then you must know what will happen to my sister's family when Elizabeth does not marry Mr. Collins."

There was motion underneath the blankets, and then the man who claimed to be Mr. Darcy pulled off a glove and extended his left hand showing the Darcy signet ring. "The care of the Bennet family will be decided between my friend and I, as Mr. Bingley has a special license to marry Miss Bennet."

Mr. Gardiner could not have been more shocked had he been struck by lightning. Mr. Bingley was a name he had heard often mentioned by his sister. Mr.

Gardiner smiled and nodded at the men. "Wait for my return with the parson."

Mr. Gardiner made haste around the outside of the church to the back door. He was gratified upon opening the door to find the parson in the sacristy. "Mr. Barrow, I have been tasked to bring you to Longbourn. I fear my niece is overcome with nerves and only a word from you will suffice."

The parson frowned and then put on his coat and hat. "I have had to comfort nervous brides a few times, though you should have come to fetch me sooner." Mr. Barrow picked up his Bible---a few readings from scripture always helped soothe nervous brides---and followed Mr. Gardiner into the Bennet carriage.

ELIZABETH'S REPRIEVE was ended by the sound of footsteps on the stairs. "Excuse me, Miss Elizabeth, but Mr. Gardiner is here with some gentlemen."

Elizabeth sat up, unsure of what she had just heard. "Did you say Mr. Gardiner and some gentlemen?"

"Yes, they are waiting downstairs for you." Hill curtsied and left the room.

Elizabeth stared at the doorway. Mr. Gardiner was supposed to take her to the church, so who were these other gentlemen? If one was Mr. Collins, surely Hill would have said so.

Elizabeth sighed and stood. It was time to do her duty. Elizabeth walked out of her bedchamber and down the stairs. She looked down the entire way to delay facing her future as long as possible. She stood on the main floor and finally looked up to see not just her uncle but Mr. Bingley, Mr. Darcy, and the parson Mr. Barrow.

Before Elizabeth could form any thought in her shocked mind, Mr. Darcy stepped forward and bowed. "Miss Bennet, I must tell you how ardently I admire you. Will you do me the great honor of becoming my wife?"

Elizabeth's astonishment was beyond expression. Mr. Darcy wanted to marry her? He ardently admired her? Her lack of appetite this sennight caught up with her though and Mr. Gardiner reached out to hold her before she fell.

Mr. Darcy continued. "If you will do me the honor of accepting my offer, I have a special license that we may be wed immediately."

Elizabeth licked her lips. She could not believe what had just occurred, that Mr. Darcy had offered his hand for her. She knew him as a proud, arrogant man that disliked George Wickham so much he left him destitute. Elizabeth stared at Mr. Darcy's handsome visage. Would marrying Mr. Darcy be better than being married to Mr. Collins?

"I thank you for the offer, Mr. Darcy, but I must know if my family will also be taken care of. Mr. Collins has vowed to turn us out if I do not marry him today."

Mr. Darcy glanced at Mr. Bingley. "Between Mr. Bingley and I, we will take care of your family."

Mr. Bingley smiled and bowed his head to Elizabeth.

Both of them? Why... did that mean that Mr. Bingley would offer for Jane? Elizabeth had questions regarding Mr. Darcy's dealings with Mr. Wickham, and reservations regarding his pride and arrogance, but Mr. Darcy was altogether a much better match for her than Mr. Collins. Her heart fluttered in her chest. "Yes, I will marry you."

Mr. Darcy smiled and offered his arm, which Elizabeth took. He then turned to face Mr. Barrow, who frowned.

"This is most irregular." He looked at Mr. Gardiner. "You brought me here under false pretenses."

Mr. Gardiner nodded. "I did. I apologize, but the subterfuge was necessary in order to prevent my niece from a future of misery."

Mr. Darcy handed a paper to the parson. "I have the special license here."

Elizabeth looked up at Mr. Darcy's profile and noticed that his skin was red in places. He still wore traveling clothes, which she just now realized were dirty in spots and wrinkled. What was the meaning of this?

"This license is legitimate. Do you have two witnesses?" Mr. Barrow looked at Mr. Darcy.

"Yes, my friend Mr. Bingley and the uncle of the bride, Mr. Gardiner."

With her stomach fluttering, and her heart beating fast, Fitzwilliam Darcy and Elizabeth Bennet were married in the drawing room of Longbourn. As she looked into his eyes, Elizabeth was surprised to find warmth and admiration. She never would have thought that Mr. Darcy held a candle for her.

Mr. Darcy slipped his signet ring onto Elizabeth's finger. It was much too big for her, but Mr. Darcy stated he would buy a wedding ring for her as soon as possible. They were pronounced man and wife, and then they kissed. Elizabeth did not know if the tingle of her lips was from her first kiss or because Mr. Darcy's lips were quite warm.

Mr. Darcy smiled and turned to his friend. "Well, Charles? It is your time now."

Mr. Bingley stepped forward to the parson. "If you would not mind staying here while I fetch my bride?"

Mr. Barrow did not have time to answer before Mr. Bingley trotted out the front door.

CHAPTER 18

Now that the wedding was over, Elizabeth felt awkward. Usually, after a wedding the happy couple walked out of the church amongst many well wishes and then rode to their new home for a wedding breakfast. But, what did one do when you were married to a different person than expected and not in the intended church?

Mr. Gardiner cleared his throat. "I could do with a spot of tea. If you would not mind, Mrs. Darcy?" Mr. Gardiner smiled genially at his niece, pleased that his address to her as Mrs. Darcy had produced a reaction in the unusually quiet Elizabeth.

"Oh, yes, we all need refreshments." Elizabeth rang for Hill and then stood and stared at the large and heavy signet ring on her left ring finger.

Mr. Darcy walked over to his bride, concerned at her thin and pale appearance and unusually quiet behavior. He could presume that some of it was due to the unexpected groom she had married, but that did not explain her wan appearance. "Elizabeth, are you unwell?"

Elizabeth turned around and almost fell. Mr. Darcy caught her in his arms and helped her walk to the closest chair. "You have been unwell. I shall have the apothecary sent for."

"No Mr. Darcy, I mean Fitzwilliam." Elizabeth looked up at him in surprise again that Mr. Darcy was her husband. "I am not unwell."

Mr. Darcy frowned at his wife. He did not recollect the Elizabeth Bennet he knew was used to stating falsehoods. He would not tolerate them either. "Mrs. Darcy, I must ask that you not tell me falsehoods. I am most concerned for your well-being."

Elizabeth pinched her lips and tilted her head up. "Mr. Darcy, it was not a falsehood and I am not in a habit of speaking falsehoods. I am not unwell. I have not eaten much this sennight and it must be due to that."

Mr. Darcy was saved from apologizing by a servant having entered the room with a tray of tea and biscuits. "Could you bring more substantial fare for Mrs. Darcy?"

Hill stared from Mr. Darcy to Elizabeth and the large ring on her left ring finger, then back to Mr. Darcy. She curtsied and said "Yes, sir."

Hill and the other servants had heard the other people arrive at Longbourn much too soon. They all stood in the hallway and listened to the wedding vows of Elizabeth Bennet and Mr. Darcy. It was one thing to eavesdrop and another to face the wedded couple in person with a signet ring on Miss Elizabeth's hand.

Hill smiled as she walked back to the kitchen. This man was much better than the greedy and cruel Mr. Collins. No girl deserved to be married to such a man as that. She knew today would probably be her last day of employment at Longbourn with the Bennets, though she was not upset about that fact. Hill did not want to stay and work for Mr. Collins.

Mr. Gardiner walked over to his niece. "You say you have not been eating this week, Elizabeth? I overheard Lydia mention---" Mr. Gardiner glanced at Mr. Darcy and realized he should not say what he had heard, especially in the presence of her new husband who already held a negative opinion of Mr. Collins.

"It is nothing. Just a bout of nerves." Elizabeth smiled and hoped this convinced her uncle to change the subject.

"I am interested in what you heard, Mr. Gardiner." Mr. Darcy stood closer to Elizabeth and stared at her uncle. Mr. Darcy's bearing was that of a man used to his orders being carried out.

Mr. Gardiner felt like he had when he was a child and was called upon to answer for his actions. "I am unsure if now is the time to discuss this."

Mr. Darcy looked around the room and saw only the parson. "I should like to hear of the treatment of my wife by her relations." He knew there had been a reason for Elizabeth's wan countenance. If Mr. Collins, her own relative, was so cruel as to throw her family out unless Elizabeth married him, what other cruelty had Mr. Collins inflicted as the master of Longbourn?

"Please Mr. Darcy, Fitzwilliam. I am embarrassed to discuss this now." Elizabeth looked up at Mr. Darcy and pleaded with her eyes.

Mr. Darcy nodded. "Very well, though we will speak of it later."

At that moment, Hill carried in a tray of stronger fare for Elizabeth to eat. So Elizabeth found herself attentively looked after by her new husband, whose conscientious and caring behavior was at odds with the arrogance she had seen herself and the stories Mr. Wickham shared.

Elizabeth finished her plate in its entirety before she heard a carriage. Elizabeth looked to Mr. Darcy. "Did I hear correctly that Mr. Bingley left to fetch his bride? Is it who I hope?"

Mr. Darcy rang the bell for a servant to remove the tray and walked back to Elizabeth with a smile. He said nothing and let the matter speak for itself as Mr. Bingley and Jane entered the drawing room. Mr. Bingley beamed, and Jane smiled but was also bewildered by the subterfuge and the sight of her sister next to Mr. Darcy.

The greetings were established, and Jane stared at the large signet ring on Elizabeth's left hand. "It is quite a surprise, is it not?" Elizabeth stood and hugged her sister.

"I found myself much surprised when Mr. Bingley came for me in the church. He said my uncle needed help with you, but then no one else was in the carriage with us. Mr. Bingley said not to worry as we were getting married immediately!"

Elizabeth squeezed her sister's arms and smiled for her with happiness. "It has been such an unexpected and yet not an unwelcome event."

"I am so glad you are smiling again, Lizzy."

Mr. Bingley turned to his intended. "Miss Bennet, we need to hurry. If you would come with me?" Mr. Bingley stuck out his arm, and both walked the short distance to where the parson now stood.

Those present had the happy duty of being witnesses for the marriage of Mr. Charles Bingley and Jane Bennet. Both beamed with joy and giggled as a ring much too big for Jane was slipped onto her left hand.

The best friends Mr. Bingley and Mr. Darcy congratulated each other on their brilliant journey and good timing while the sisters hugged each other and their uncle.

Mr. Gardiner was intrigued by the men's mention of a journey and good timing, but he had the wherewithal to realize that they needed to hurry from Longbourn before Mr. Collins found out that his bride was no longer unwed. "I hesitate to stop the celebration, but I feel we must quit Longbourn with haste. It has been some time since I left with the parson. I am not sure how much longer we have before someone comes."

Elizabeth's smile fell. "How much time do you think we have? I fear Jane and I will not be allowed back at Longbourn once we leave."

Mr. Darcy turned to Elizabeth. "You may have enough time to grab only the essentials that cannot be replaced. Clothing and books can all be purchased anew."

Elizabeth smiled at her husband, still shocked by the turn of events that day, then turned to rush up the stairs followed by Jane. They both entered their bedchamber, and Elizabeth looked at the room with new eyes. "I am not sure there is anything that I cannot replace, except for the necklace Papa gave me and my favorite books."

"Lizzy, you can replace books. We need to hurry. I do not want to be here when Mr. Collins finds out that you married someone else." Elizabeth looked back at Jane, and both of them giggled.

"No, I cannot imagine Mr. Collins will be happy with that information." Elizabeth packed her walking shoes, the little jewelry she owned, a few books, and her half-mourning dresses.

Jane packed much the same except for fewer books. "Lizzy, your wedding dress is in the box."

Elizabeth turned to Jane. "I was not going to wear it. I was going to wear black for my wedding to Mr. Collins in memory of Papa and because I was forced. And now I do not want to see that wedding dress ever again."

Elizabeth and Jane quickly went down the stairs and carried the trunk between them until the men took it out of their hands.

"Oh, wait! I want something of Papa's. I will be right back."

Elizabeth ran to Mr. Bennet's study but could not open the door. It was locked. She pounded the door. "Blast you, Mr. Collins!"

"Elizabeth?" Mr. Darcy turned around the corner.

Elizabeth turned to Mr. Darcy while tears fell out of her eyes. "Mr. Collins has locked the door again. All of Papa's books and trinkets are in there. I just wanted something, a memento to have of him." Elizabeth choked back a sob.

"I am sorry. Is there nothing of his elsewhere that you can take quickly?"

Elizabeth shook her head. She wiped the tears off her face. "No, he kept everything in his study. Mr. Collins locked it right after he came so that we could not take anything away that---" Elizabeth stopped as she realized what she had been saying.

"I am very interested to hear how he has been treating you. But now is not the time. We must leave."

Elizabeth looked up at her husband and made the decision to be far away from Longbourn before Mr. Darcy found out how she had been treated. She knew Mr. Collins had a temper, and she did not want her new husband to be injured so soon after he had just saved her.

Mr. Gardiner turned around the corner. "Elizabeth, we must leave!"

Mr. Darcy held Elizabeth's arm and led them out of Longbourn. Their trunk was already situated on one carriage with Mr. and Mrs. Bingley inside the carriage.

Mr. Gardiner turned to Mr. Darcy. "I shall get in this carriage and take the parson back to the church. You should go to your home directly."

Mr. Darcy frowned at Mr. Gardiner. "That sounds quite reasonable, except you should not be the one to bear the brunt of Mr. Collins' ire. I would not leave you to face him alone. We will follow you to the church."

CHAPTER 19

Mrs. Bennet was restless in the pew at the church. She was sure their family was the laughingstock of everyone in Meryton with her daughter's refusal to come to her own wedding. First her brother was sent to fetch her, then Jane. Where could they be? When Elizabeth finally showed, she was going to hear from her. Mrs. Bennet was sure that the parson, Mr. Barrow was well in his cups by now in the sacristy and would be unfit to even marry them when her recalcitrant daughter finally arrived.

Mrs. Bennet glanced at the first pew to Mr. Collins, whose countenance was quite the opposite of what one would expect on a groom's wedding day. He had been all courteous and kindness, but now sat in the first pew faced straight ahead. His countenance was such a color that Mrs. Bennet worried, or hoped, that he would suffer an apoplexy.

Mrs. Bennet did not want to turn around to look at the friends who had come to support her this day. She had been so relieved and happy when she had invited them to the wedding, but now greatly regretted the invitations to the Lucas and Long families. She could not imagine what they thought, but could hear their murmurs.

She leaned over to her eldest daughter in the pew. "Mary, go outside and see if they have arrived."

Mary continued to look forward and then glanced at her mother. "I am sure Elizabeth is being difficult. They will be here soon. I do not see why I need to stand in the cold to watch for their arrival."

Mrs. Bennet dug her hands into Mary's arm. "You will go outside and see if the carriage has arrived! If it has not, we will have to think of something. We cannot be thrown out of our home and left destitute because of that obstinate, headstrong girl."

Mary squeezed in front of Kitty and Lydia to exit the pew and walk down the side aisle. The murmuring in the church ceased. Mrs. Bennet pretended not to notice and instead checked the feathers on her hat and coat. She glanced up at Mr. Collins to find him turned towards the front of the church with a glare. Mrs. Bennet quickly looked back down.

If her foolish daughter did not show, she would have to send one of her other daughters to marry in Elizabeth's place. If only they could get a marriage license that quickly, and if Mr. Collins agreed. She did not know what else they would do. Her family could not all live with the Phillips or the Gardiners. This was their only chance. That child had better not ruin their future due to her selfishness.

Mrs. Bennet leaned over to her sister-in-law, Mrs. Gardiner. "I cannot imagine my brother would have difficulty convincing Elizabeth to leave. I would think she had enough reason and sense to know that her behavior is unseemly, and this shall be a scandal for quite some time not only affecting her but the rest of us as well!"

Mrs. Gardiner turned to Mrs. Bennet but did not know what to say that she had not already said. It was a horrible situation that the Bennets had been put in due to Mr. Bennet, and it was dreadfully unfair to Elizabeth.

The murmuring in the church grew louder, so Mrs. Bennet pretended to fix her hat and took a look back to see the Longs leaving the church. She quickly turned forward, mortified. She hoped Mr. Collins did not see this, for he might refuse to marry Elizabeth even after she came to the church. Then, where would they be? Thrown out on the streets begging for scraps of food! It was too late though as she saw Mr. Collins stand, then march to the back of the church and open the doors.

"Oh, we are ruined. Sister, what shall we do? We will have nowhere to live, we will be thrown out! Blast that obstinate girl. I should go to Longbourn and drag her out myself." Mrs. Bennet clenched her fists.

Mrs. Gardiner reached for Mrs. Bennet's arm, but missed as Mrs. Bennet stood, stepped around her to exit the pew and then stormed down the aisle to follow Mr. Collins out the front doors of the church. That was a sign for the rest of the attendees to also stand and leave the church. It was a great noise with all the talk of the shocking scandal that Elizabeth Bennet did not show at her own wedding.

Mrs. Bennet hurried after Mr. Collins who stood with clenched fists and stared down the lane. "Oh, Mr. Collins, you know how Elizabeth can be. I will go and talk to her and bring her to the church. Do not leave! I will bring her back right away and this will be all straightened out. You will be married soon."

Mr. Collins turned to Mrs. Bennet who stepped back at the ferocity of his countenance. "Madam, I have been made a fool of. I have stood at the front of that church for a bride that has not shown. I have been made the laughingstock of this village all due to Elizabeth Bennet! No, I will not marry her anymore and furthermore you are all to leave Longbourn immediately!"

Mrs. Bennet gasped. This was far worse than anything she could have imagined. "Oh, please no Mr. Collins, you cannot do this. Elizabeth will marry you; I will force her. I will get her right away." Mrs. Bennet walked quickly towards Longbourn with Mrs. Phillips. They were forced off the lane as carriages rapidly approached the church.

Mrs. Bennet recognized their carriage, but it was followed by another carriage covered with enough snow that she could not make out the ownership. But Mrs. Bennet did not care about that second carriage, only the first.

"She is here, she is here! Mr. Collins! Mr. Collins, Elizabeth is here now!" Mrs. Bennet quickly walked back to the church.

The first carriage door opened and the Meryton church parson Mr. Barrow descended. Mr. Gardiner climbed out after him. He walked to his wife, now outside with all the wedding attendees, but Mrs. Bennet approached him and grabbed his arm. "Brother, why do you not have Elizabeth?"

Mr. Gardiner turned toward his sister and saw over her shoulder the ferocious countenance of Mr. Collins bearing down on them. "Where is my cousin, Elizabeth? I have waited and waited at the front of the church! I have been humiliated and mortified and I will not wait one minute more! This is not seemly for a man of my standing with Lady Catherine de Bourgh as my patroness, and I, the master of Longbourn, to be treated in such a horrible manner by that worthless girl!" Mr. Collins spit his last words out to the disgust of those who stood near.

Mr. Gardiner drew himself up. "Now see here, Mr. Collins, you are discussing my niece. You will not talk about her in that language in front of me."

"I shall discuss her in the language that fits! Your niece is a horrible woman. An obstinate, recalcitrant girl that is worthy of nothing but to live on the streets and beg for scraps from her betters, which is exactly where she will be when I throw the entire family out of Longbourn!"

Cries of astonishment were raised throughout the crowd surrounding the small party. Mrs. Bennet was mortified that all the wedding attendees and several of the villagers watched the spectacle in front of the church. She covered her face and looked around for her other daughters. "Oh brother, sister, I am having such aches and pains. Such fluttering of my nerves! We must leave. Find my girls, I need to lie down."

The door of the second carriage suddenly opened as a footman pulled down the steps. Mr. Darcy stepped out of the carriage. The crowd went quiet. Mr. Collins was also struck speechless and could only stare in wonder at the nephew of his patroness.

"Mr. Collins, I could not help but overhear your comments, so loud they were stated. I will not allow you to speak of my wife in that manner."

There was absolute silence and then what Mr. Darcy had stated finally registered. The noise of all the wedding attendees and crowd of villagers talked at once. No one could be heard such was the chaos at the shocking pronouncement. Mr. Collins stood and gaped like a fish.

Mr. Darcy turned to the carriage and held out his arm. A woman's hand reached out, and then Elizabeth showed and climbed out of the carriage to join her husband. She smiled at the gathered crowd.

Mr. Darcy turned and addressed them. "I apologize for you came to the church to witness a wedding, but the wedding was held elsewhere. May I present my wife, Mrs. Elizabeth Bennet Darcy." Mr. Darcy stared directly at Mr. Collins.

The exclamations and astonishment of the crowd were such that it was complete pandemonium. Mrs. Bennet turned to her brother and sister and then back to the couple in front of the carriage. "Do you see this, brother and sister? Mr. Darcy! I knew nothing, and he has 10,000 pounds a year!"

Mr. Collins was decidedly not overcome with joy for the shocking development. He pushed and shoved his way to the happy couple without care. "You have stolen my wife!"

Mr. Collins pointed his finger right at Mr. Darcy, unable to speak again, such was his rage.

Elizabeth took a step back and stood half-shielded by her husband's body.

Mr. Darcy was not cowed, though. "I have done no such thing. Elizabeth accepted my offer, and we were married."

"You cannot be married legally though. You did not get married in the church, nor did you have the banns read! You are at fault of the marriage law of---"

"We were legally married by special license by Mr. Barrow this morning at Longbourn. Mr. Barrow has the legal document if you would like to inspect it, Mr. Collins, though you will find everything completed satisfactorily." Mr. Darcy's usual stern visage displayed a small smirk at saving his beloved from the odious, unscrupulous toad.

"I demand satisfaction! You have humiliated me in front of the entire village that I live in! You have stolen my wife and you will pay."

Exclamations ran through the crowd. No one in Meryton had ever witnessed one gentleman call another out, but they had read of it in the papers.

"Mr. Collins, you are a man of the cloth. I daresay you cannot call another gentleman out for a duel." Though Mr. Darcy was quite sure Mr. Collins was bluffing, he was gratified to feel Elizabeth clutch his arm even tighter.

Elizabeth did not want to lose her gallant savior so soon after he rescued her. "Please no, Mr. Darcy. You cannot get hurt!"

Mr. Darcy turned to Elizabeth. "Do not worry, my dear. I am quite proficient with the sword and pistol."

Mr. Barrow was finally able to make his way over to his fellow man of the church. "Mr. Collins! Pull yourself together. This is not the behavior of a man of the church. Come into the parsonage with me---"

Mr. Collins turned towards the clergyman and pushed him away to the gasps of the crowd. "I will not! You were part of this. You helped that man, that man that coveted my bride, to steal her from me!" He turned back to Mr. Darcy. "I demand satisfaction! Name your second."

Mr. Darcy stared at Mr. Collins, then looked him up and down. "It is illegal to duel and I will not be part of it. I will also not point a weapon at a man of the church, no matter how lacking he is in regard to the rules of the church."

This set down in front of the attendees for his wedding and numerous Meryton villagers struck Mr. Collins so severely that he was unable to speak. He shook with clenched fists and a vermilion countenance so fierce that a ring of empty space surrounded him.

Mr. Darcy turned back to the second carriage and conversed with someone inside before he turned back to the crowd. "I have the great honor of announcing that my wedding was not the only one that took place this morning at Longbourn."

Mr. Bingley climbed out of the carriage. He beamed with delight and held out his hand as Jane climbed down from the carriage. Mr. Bingley could barely be heard over the exclamations of the crowd. "May I introduce my wife, Mrs. Jane Bennet Bingley."

The crowd rushed forward again to greet the second newly married couple of the day. They flowed around Mr. Collins as if he was an easily ignored obstacle, which did not help his temper in the slightest.

Mrs. Bennet's screech was quite loud, but Mr. Gardiner's arm prevented her from running towards her daughter. "Franny, we must leave now. Get in the first carriage. We must leave before Mr. Collins finds us."

Mrs. Bennet struggled to pull her arm away. "I must go see Jane and Mr. Bingley! You cannot deny me my right as mother of the bride to congratulate her."

Mrs. Gardiner held Mrs. Bennet's other arm and helped her husband pull Mrs. Bennet towards the first carriage. "Sister, Mr. Collins will not take this well. I fear for you and the girls if you stay here too long. You must leave now. Where are your other daughters?"

Mrs. Bennet finally realized what the Gardiners had said. "You do not think that Mr. Collins would hurt us? He would never do such a thing. He has been most kind and attentive to us." But she did look around for the three girls. "I cannot see them. I sent

Mary out to the front of the church, but I do not know where Kitty and Lydia are. You are incorrect though, he would not hurt us. It is Elizabeth he is angry with, and rightly so."

Mr. Gardiner knew his sister well, yet he was still disgusted. "Francine! Get in the carriage and stay inside. I will find the girls." He handed Mrs. Bennet and his wife into the first carriage and closed the door.

CHAPTER 20

Mr. Collins stood at the back of the crowd that surrounded the happy couples. His fists were clenched, and he was wearing a countenance that was far removed from what one would expect the countenance of a parson would be.

Lydia pushed her way through the people that surrounded the newly wedded couples. "Jane! Jane! You got married! Is this not exciting? You must have a large ball to celebrate at Netherfield! Oh, but we are in mourning and cannot go to a ball."

Mr. Collins spied Lydia as she pushed her way past him to get close to the eldest Bennet girl who had married this morning, in another wedding held at Longbourn, his estate, without him in attendance! While he was at the church, while he waited for his bride, they both got married to other men!

Mr. Collins eyes narrowed, and he grabbed Lydia. "You must show some decorum and propriety for the situation. It is reprehensible how the Bennet girls have been allowed to run wild. I have seen how you have acted at the balls and dinner parties, and I am ashamed at being a relation of yours!"

Lydia turned towards Mr. Collins. "Get your hands off me!"

Mr. Collins looked back at the crowd and noticed people looking back at the commotion. Mr. Collins smiled and nodded. "I apologize for the censure of my cousin's wild behavior. I do not want to upset the happiness and felicitations of my dear cousins."

The people that had been alarmed were now consoled and turned back to the newly-wedded couples.

Mr. Collins dug his fingers in her arm and dragged her back towards the church. Lydia struggled as he dragged her through the doors of the church.

"Stop! What are you doing? Get your hands off me! You dirty deviant! I told Mama something was wrong with you."

Mr. Collins recoiled from a kick that landed directly on his shin. Before Lydia could run, he wrapped his arms around her, covered her mouth and dragged her back to the sacristy. Mr. Barrow was employed at putting things from the cancelled wedding away.

"Mr. Barrow, if I may trouble you to officiate a wedding yet today? I shall marry this Bennet girl, instead."

Lydia stopped her struggles, her eyes wide with shock at his pronouncement. Mr. Collins dropped his hand from her mouth before Mr. Barrow turned. The parson saw a smiling Mr. Collins and a shocked bride who did not seem to be there through any coercion.

"Mr. Collins, this is most irregular. You must have a license to marry or have the banns read for three weeks. You know this." Mr. Barrow glanced at Lydia as she began her struggles again. She pushed against Mr. Collins, though she could not budge. "And, I daresay Miss Lydia Bennet is under the age of ten and six, and would need her uncle's permission."

Mr. Collins leaned forward and smiled. "I have the license here, as you can see, Mr. Barrow."

Mr. Collins handed a paper to Mr. Barrow, who opened the marriage license and examined it. It was easy for him to read the name of Mr. Collins, but the first name of the bride was difficult to make out, though the surname of Bennet was easy to read. "Why is it difficult to read the bride's first name?"

"The bishop is quite old and his hand shakes a bit. You see there it says Lydia Bennet and there is a signature by Mr. Edward Gardiner."

Mr. Barrow examined the license. He had enough money now, but this was an opportunity to earn more. He had earned quite more than the usual ten guineas for a wedding this morning from Mr. Darcy and Mr. Bingley. For this wedding, he was sure he would only receive ten guineas from Mr. Collins.

Mr. Barrow glanced up at Mr. Collins and considered his career if he turned down this request from him. Mr. Collins was well connected with Lady Catherine de Bourgh, and he did not want to draw ire from that direction. Yet when he glanced at Lydia Bennet, he was certain she was not an entirely willing participant.

"Mr. Collins, I would feel much better about this situation if Mr. Gardiner were here to witness. You will need another witness as well."

Mr. Collins nodded. "Oh yes, yes. You are quite right, Mr. Barrow. I shall fetch them directly." Mr. Collins bowed, then pulled Lydia with him while she continued to struggle and push at him.

"You are balmy if you think I am going to marry you!" said Lydia. "No one has to marry you now, for Mr. Darcy and Mr. Bingley will take care of us. We do not need you anymore."

Mr. Collins stopped and pulled Lydia harshly to him, and she cried out in pain. "Be quiet. I could still throw you and your family out of Longbourn. Do not tempt me, for I have seen the way you run about and look at the officers and men. Do you want me to tell Mrs. Bennet what I saw you doing with an officer behind the shops? Your reputation will be ruined then, Lydia Bennet. No one will have you and you will be thrown out. Not even Mr. Darcy or Mr. Bingley will be able to help you then." Mr. Collins pulled a suddenly-compliant Lydia with him as he went outside to find Mrs. Bennet and Mr. Gardiner.

Mrs. Bennet had climbed out of the carriage and stood next to her favorite daughter Jane and new son-in-law Mr. Bingley. She beamed with joy from the felicitations of the Long and Lucas families, as well as the large crowd of Meryton villagers that had continued to grow as the word of the shocking developments had spread. The Bennet family had been referred to as most unlucky and now were regarded as the luckiest family in Hertfordshire for the marriage of two Bennet daughters to the richest men any had known.

Mr. Collins sidled up to Mrs. Bennet and leaned down. "Mrs. Bennet, you are needed in the church."

Mrs. Bennet turned to Mr. Collins with annoyance. "What am I needed for? There is nothing to do."

"You are needed as I would like to marry my cousin Lydia, however she is presenting difficulties."

"Oh! Three daughters married in one day? Yes, I will come, but wait, do we not need my brother?"

"Yes, he must witness. Will you bring him into the church?" Mr. Collins smiled at Mrs. Bennet.

Mrs. Bennet found her brother by the carriage. "Brother, do come into the church. There is a matter that needs our attention yet."

Mr. Gardiner frowned at his sister. "Franny, I told you to get into the carriage. We do not--"

"Do not worry about that, Mr. Collins needs us in the church. He is to marry Lydia and you must witness the marriage." Mrs. Bennet turned and beamed at the thought of yet another daughter married.

"Mr. Collins to marry Lydia? But she is not yet six and ten." Mrs. Gardiner stuck her head out of the carriage and watched Mrs. Bennet enter the church.

Mr. Gardiner turned back to his wife. "I do not like the sounds of this. Hurry!"

Mr. Barrow walked out of the sacristy doorway. "Mr. Collins, I see you have Mrs. Bennet; however, you still need the head of the Bennet family."

Mr. and Mrs. Gardiner entered the church. "I heard that Mr. Collins will marry Lydia."

"Yes! I shall have three married and on the same day!" Mrs. Bennet held Lydia's arm.

Mrs. Gardiner was quite concerned, as she had not seen any sign of affection in Lydia for Mr. Collins, nor did she think this an appropriate match for a girl to a man not of the best character, according to her husband.

"I would like to talk with my niece before the wedding." Mr. Gardiner held out his arm for Lydia to follow him, but Mrs. Bennet held onto her arm while Mr. Collins held her other arm. "Lydia? I would like to speak with you."

CHAPTER 21

"I do not want to marry Mr. Collins! He said he would turn us all out of Longbourn if I did not marry him, but I do not want to! There is no need for any of us to marry him as Mr. Bingley and Mr. Darcy said they would take care of us now!" She punctuated her last words by pulling her arms out of the holds of Mrs. Bennet and Mr. Collins, who were too shocked to hold on to her.

"Now Lydia, calm down," said Mrs. Bennet. "It is a very advantageous match and you can still live in Longbourn---"

"Mr. Collins," said Mr. Barrow, "I cannot perform this wedding as the bride does not agree and has indeed firmly stated that she does not wish to marry you." Mr. Barrow nodded to those gathered, then walked back into the sacristy and closed the door.

Lydia turned to Mrs. Bennet. "I will never be nice to you again! You tried to force me to marry that dirty deviant." Lydia stormed out of the church.

Mrs. Bennet turned, glanced at her brother and sister in law, fluttered her handkerchief with pursed lips, and then quit the church. Mr. Gardiner turned his wife with raised eyebrows, and then they both quit the church as well.

Mrs. Phillips grabbed ahold of her sister as she walked towards the newlyweds. "What shall you do about the wedding breakfast? It cannot be held at Longbourn anymore."

"I know, sister, I know! I do not know what to do. That child has ruined everything. Now we shall be thrown out of our only home and I have been made a laughingstock of Meryton!"

Mr. Collins passed them without a glance and walked towards Longbourn.

Mr. Bingley addressed the friends and relatives gathered. "All are welcome to come to Netherfield Park." He nodded to Mr. Darcy and then handed Jane into the carriage. Elizabeth and Mr. Darcy climbed in next.

The carriage jerked forward and soon settled in to a swaying motion as the horses trotted to Netherfield Park. Their new home was further from Meryton than Longbourn. Elizabeth thought with some sadness that she might not get to ramble upon her favorite paths on the grounds of Longbourn to walk up Oakham Mount anymore. However, she was gratified that she was not married to Mr. Collins and was not subject to her mother's whims anymore.

Elizabeth glanced to her right at Mr. Darcy, who looked forward with his hands rested on his thighs. She could never have imagined this day to turn out the way it had. She had thought Mr. Darcy a proud and arrogant man, one that did not find her tolerable enough to tempt him, but something had changed as he had offered for her that morning. No man would have offered nor married a woman they did not like, especially if it was to save her from a marriage to an odious man.

Mr. Darcy's actions that day were quite at odds with what she had seen of him before, and with what George Wickham had said. Elizabeth did not know her husband well at all, and she was nervous about that fact. She needed time to learn about her new husband. The only facts she knew were that he lived in Derbyshire; had 10,000 pounds a year; had a younger sister; and that George Wickham was the son of the late Mr. Darcy's steward. That was definitely not enough to start a marriage with, but she was still grateful for Mr. Darcy's timely intervention.

Elizabeth smiled at the happy couple that sat across from her. Mr. Bingley and Jane shared small smiles and blushes, and both beamed with true love. Elizabeth was so relieved and happy that Jane and Mr. Bingley were married. She did not know what the future held for her, but she knew it was the start of an adventure.

Elizabeth looked to her right and found Mr. Darcy's gaze already upon her. She almost looked down but stopped herself to hold his stare and give him a small smile. A smile also formed on his face.

Their carriage rolled to a stop in front of Netherfield. As the hall was leased by Mr. Bingley, the Bingleys climbed out of the carriage first, then the Darcys. As Elizabeth stepped off the bottom step, a patch of snow fell off the carriage to land near her feet. She exclaimed and looked at the inches of snow that coated the carriage.

She turned back to Mr. Darcy, who stood waiting for her with his arm cocked. "Your carriage is covered under a thick layer of snow. Did you ride through that storm the day before?"

"I shall tell you all later, but right now we have guests and relatives to see to."

Elizabeth put her arm on his and they walked up the steps to the front door. The only way that carriage could be covered in that much snow was if they had driven through the snowstorm the day before. Had they gone to London for a special license just yesterday? Elizabeth could not wait to hear the story.

They entered Netherfield to hear Mr. Bingley give orders to his valet that he needed to speak to his housekeeper immediately as they expected a party of people for a wedding breakfast. "This is my wife, Mrs. Jane Bingley."

Mr. Bingley's valet was surprised, but bowed to his mistress and carried on with his duties as a good valet should.

Miss Bingley wandered into the entryway, having just missed her brother's announcement. "Charles? And Mr. Darcy? I thought you were to be in London for days. You surely did not have enough time to run all our errands."

"We did not, Caroline. May I present to you my wife, Mrs. Jane Bingley?"

Miss Bingley's countenance fell, as well as her hands that had been clasped in front of her. She stared at her brother and his new wife without a word.

"Caroline!" Mr. Bingley censured his sister, which was new behavior for him and further upset Miss Bingley.

"Pardon me." Miss Bingley curtsied to her new sister, but that did not quiet her for long. "Married? Why, how is that possible? You left for London yesterday." By this time, Mrs. Louisa Hurst had also wandered into the entryway.

"Married? Who is married?" Mrs. Hurst had better manners than her sister and curtsied to the group in greeting.

"I have just informed Caroline that I have married this morning. I would like to present my wife, Mrs. Jane Bingley."

Mrs. Hurst was better at the concealment of her emotions. She smiled, curtsied and welcomed the new Mrs. Bingley to the family. She then turned to Mr. Darcy with a quick look up and down of Elizabeth's black mourning dress.

"I was not the only one that got married this morning," Mr. Bingley announced while he looked at Mr. Darcy with a smile.

Mr. Darcy looked at Elizabeth as he announced, "May I present my wife, Mrs. Elizabeth Darcy."

He then turned to the Bingley sisters to see that neither one of them could hide their reaction. Mr. Darcy scowled at the twin looks of horror.

CHAPTER 22

"Married? You have married?" Miss Bingley stepped back and brought her hand up to her throat. She was of such pale color that Elizabeth wondered if she would swoon and if anyone would bother to catch her.

"Miss Bingley, Mrs. Hurst, if you would do the honor of acknowledging my wife?" Mr. Darcy was not cowed in the slightest by the Bingley sisters, unlike his friend. It was much easier to manage headstrong woman if you were not related to them.

The Bingley sisters gave perfunctory curtsies. Miss Bingley mentioned something about a sudden headache and left to go upstairs to her bedchamber.

Mrs. Hurst excused herself to look on her sister and left as well.

Mr. Bingley scowled at where his sisters had exited.

Elizabeth was not surprised at all by their reaction. Actually, it had gone better than she had thought it would. "Having their brother come home unexpectedly married must have been quite a shock for them."

Mr. Bingley turned to Elizabeth with a smile. "Yes, yes indeed, it had to have been. But I am not any less happy for it." He beamed at Jane.

The housekeeper, Mrs. Pond, quickly walked over to Mr. Bingley and studied what she had heard was the new mistress of the house. Introductions were made, and the housekeeper was eager to meet with the new Mrs. Bingley whenever she would like to have a tour of the house and look over the menus.

"Thank you, Mrs. Pond. I shall enjoy that, but for now we need food prepared as a group of relatives and friends are arriving soon for a wedding breakfast. Do not take undo trouble for an elaborate menu, just whatever you can prepare quickly. I understand this is a last-minute request."

"Oh yes, indeed," said Mr. Bingley, "do not overtax yourselves at all. I daresay whatever Cook makes will be wonderful. We would like some refreshments brought up soon though for when the guests arrive."

Mrs. Pond curtsied and left to give the orders to the kitchen staff. They would be gratified to know that the new mistress was the same sweet Bennet girl that had been ill and stayed at Netherfield for several days. Hopefully that sweet girl had enough starch in her back to take on Miss Bingley. It would certainly save Mrs. Pond the task of finding new staff as they quit or were fired by Miss Bingley.

The newly wedded couples did not have much time to themselves before the arrival of relatives began. The Bennet carriage arrived first with Mrs. Bennet, Lydia, Kitty, Mary and the Gardiners. It was good that the Bingley sisters were not in attendance, as this would have pushed them quite over the edge.

Mrs. Bennet walked into the sitting room and gushed with pride. "Jane, you look at home here at Netherfield. What a fine home you have, perfect for a growing family."

Elizabeth blushed and hoped her mother meant the possibility of Jane soon carrying a child and not the fact that the Bennet family would move in.

"Oh, Jane and Lizzy," said Lydia, "you have to have a wedding ball now! You cannot get married without a wedding ball especially when you have such a fine big house such as this. You must invite all the officers, as what is a ball without regimentals?" Lydia threw herself down on a sofa like Elizabeth had seen her do at Longbourn.

"Lydia! We are still in mourning for Papa." Elizabeth frowned at her youngest sister.

The next group that entered the room, Mr. and Mrs. Gardiner brought a smile to Elizabeth's visage. Elizabeth stood and exchanged greetings. Mr. and Mrs. Phillips also gave their greetings, then immediately went to Mrs. Bennet's side. They were much too in awe of the grand wealthy men that their nieces had married to partake in conversation with them.

Elizabeth was comfortable with this arrangement as she had the happy knowledge that these relations would not mortify her. It was with surprise Elizabeth found out her aunt grew up in Derbyshire not far from Pemberley the estate that Mr. Darcy owned.

Their conversation moved along pleasantly, aside from raucous laughter from Lydia and exclamations from Mrs. Bennet.

Refreshments soon arrived, which caused Mrs. Bennet to exclaim over the French cooks that Mr. Bingley probably had, and the level of dining and wondrous meals, and things that Jane would now be able to afford. Elizabeth closed her eyes every time Mrs. Bennet made a loud declaration that showed everyone where Lydia learned her behavior.

They were called into the dining room for the wedding breakfast, which amazed Elizabeth. "Charles, Jane, I must commend you on what a fine kitchen staff you have. Such a wondrous feast prepared on last-minute notice."

Both smiled, though Mr. Bingley beamed. "Thank you, sister. I daresay I have the best staff. I could not find a happier or more industrious staff anywhere in England."

The wedding breakfast cut down on the exclamations from Mrs. Bennet as she was busy eating. What was notable was the arrival of the Hursts and Miss Bingley. They did not converse with anyone, but shared many looks with each other. Elizabeth did not look forward to spending any time around those women, but now that this was her home for the time being, she would have to make do.

~

Mr. Collins stepped into the entryway of Longbourn and slammed the door. He stood with wet shoes in his Sunday best when Hill and the other servants rushed into the entry hall. Their smiles faded as they saw Mr. Collins was alone and not a happy man. The servants scattered like mice, however their flight was short-lived.

"I want everything that belongs to those blasted Bennets thrown out!" Mr. Collins stepped forward and realized it felt good to yell. "I want everything of theirs, any personal effects, clothes, novels to be thrown out at once!"

Breathing heavily, Mr. Collins stomped down the hallway to his study. He removed the key, unlocked and opened the door then stormed inside. He poured himself a healthy drink of brandy and drank it. He looked at the glass, then threw it in the fireplace.

He walked around the study until he spied a vase. He picked it up, raised it over his head, and smashed it in pieces on the floor. Anything that could break, he picked up and threw. Nothing escaped his destruction. Mr. Collins left the furniture itself alone as chairs and side tables were necessary, but anything he deemed extravagant was smashed. Mr. Collins made his way through the main floor of the house in this fashion.

He then went upstairs to the girls' rooms. He passed the doors until he stood in front of the elder Bennet girls' room. He walked into the room and spied the silver-backed handheld mirror. He smashed it on the floor. Mr. Collins pulled open a dresser drawer, but shut the first drawer as those looked like Jane's dresses. He pulled open the next drawer and smiled at the dresses therein that had been worn by Elizabeth. He pulled them out and tore every single one of them to shreds.

He stopped to take stock and realized he had accidentally shredded every dress that had been in the dresser, even those that were Jane's. He shrugged. She had married Mr. Bingley; she could afford new clothing. He had made quite a mess, but he felt good. It was about time he let go of his anger in this manner. He had run out of vases a long time ago at the Hunsford parsonage and had found it difficult to continue buying vases when he only had one or two of them to show at any time. His ire currently satisfied, Mr. Collins turned to find the servants scurry away from him again.

"Clean this mess up immediately. Throw the clothing out and burn it."

Mr. Collins walked downstairs into the study and carried the bottle of brandy and one lone glass out. He sat in the drawing room, opened his copy of Fordyce's Sermons, drank his brandy and read while his servants cleaned up the destruction he had wrought on Longbourn.

CHAPTER 23

Miss Bingley excused herself from the wedding breakfast with a significant look at her sister. She ignored any servants in her path as she stormed upstairs to her bedchamber and slammed the door. She did not care if the sound carried throughout the house, even to those still in the dining room who celebrated that travesty of a wedding. Two weddings, lest she forget that her Mr. Darcy had married that Elizabeth Bennet.

"It is insupportable! How dare he do this? What happened to their trip to London?" Miss Bingley did not know how her brother had gotten out from under their control. The sisters had had everything the way they had wanted it. Miss Bingley was mistress of her brother's home; she had a healthy allowance and invitations to all the best parties and balls in town. The only problem she had before was Mr. Bingley constantly moving about the country as he looked for the perfect estate to buy.

But, this was the absolute worst. One could not plumb the depths of how wretchedly horrible this turn of events was. And, for Mr. Darcy to be married as well. The seventh circle of hell could not be worse than what she currently experienced in this backwards county of Hertfordshire. And, for her brother to actually marry one of them? "A stupid country girl that probably only knows how to smile!"

A quick knock on the door and then Mrs. Hurst entered. "I see you have started already. What are we going to do, Caroline? Charles married! And now the Bennets are to invade Netherfield! It is enough to make me want to return to town, and you know how I hate that foul London air." Mrs. Hurst flounced onto on a sitting chair and scowled.

Miss Bingley continued to pace. "I cannot believe our brother went and did something like this, Louisa. Whatever gave him the idea that he could just ask someone to marry him? Without even our approval? Without consideration to her family, her relations, her connections?"

Mrs. Hurst nodded. "It is very selfish of him. I admit Jane is a beautiful girl, but her mother! Are we to be forced to listen to the constant brazen and presumptuous display of Mrs. Bennet crowing about her good fortune to have two daughters married to rich men?"

"Not only do we have Mrs. Bennet," said Miss Bingley, "but we have all the daughters as well! The youngest says whatever is on her mind. Did you see her, Caroline? She could not even sit properly for the propriety of a formal dining room!" Miss Bingley collapsed into another armchair.

The sisters stared despondently at the fire. "I fear Mr. Darcy is much to blame for this." Miss Bingley looked at Mrs. Hurst in shock. "No, Caroline, hear me out. I know you favor or had favored Mr. Darcy, but he is much too strong-minded for Charles. He has obviously rubbed off on him in a bad way."

Miss Bingley wanted to defend Mr. Darcy, but after he went and married that country hoyden Elizabeth Bennet, she did not currently have a favorable impression of him.

THE HAPPY BUT tired couples stood in the entryway as the last relative left Netherfield and the footman closed the door. Elizabeth turned and smiled at Jane. At least they did not have to go through this alone. They were together at Netherfield and they could face the Bingley sisters together.

Mrs. Bennet stood in the entryway with the couples. "Oh, what a delightful wedding breakfast that was. Such fine foods. Mrs. Long could not stop gushing about how lucky you two girls are."

Mrs. Bennet smiled, flicked her handkerchief, and then exclaimed, "Well, we shall leave for Longbourn. Mr. Collins said that he would throw us out if Elizabeth did not marry him, but I do not think he will do that." Mrs. Bennet turned back towards the game room and called for the youngest Bennets.

ELIZABETH STOOD in the upstairs hall and watched Jane and Mr. Bingley walk into their bedchamber. Here was the stark difference between the two marriages---Jane and Mr. Bingley knew and cared for each other, but Elizabeth and Mr. Darcy did not. Elizabeth shivered as she realized what tonight meant.

"Elizabeth?" Mr. Darcy stood in front of the open door to his bedchamber.

She swallowed, gave a small smile and walked past him into their shared room. She had always imagined her wedding day would differ greatly from this. She thought she would know, respect, and approve of her husband. Not that she was not grateful that Mr. Darcy was her husband instead of Mr. Collins. She shuddered again.

"Are you cold? I will call the servant to add more wood to the fire." Mr. Darcy's attention also disproved the impression she had formed of him.

"Oh no, Mr. Darcy, I did not shiver due to cold."

Mr. Darcy turned towards her. "As we are now married, would you do me the honor of calling me Fitzwilliam?"

Elizabeth blushed. It embarrassed her how badly she was performing as his wife. "I am sorry for not doing so."

Mr. Darcy put his hands behind his back. "It is understandable. You have had quite a day."

Elizabeth blushed anew under his scrutiny. She had so many things on her mind now compared to the past sennight, when she had only thought of how to survive. She did not want Mr. Darcy to regret the hasty marriage and petition for an annulment. Elizabeth wanted to do everything perfectly to please him, and yet she had mis-stepped already. How could she not even think to call him by his first name?

Elizabeth looked down as she spun Mr. Darcy's large signet ring around her finger.

"Pardon me, Elizabeth. I should have given you this sooner, but I wanted to do it in private."

He held out his hand. Elizabeth looked up at him with a furrowed brow.

"Your left hand, Elizabeth."

Elizabeth blushed again and put her left hand in his. He slid his signet ring off Elizabeth's finger, pulled a small gold band out of his pocket, and slid it on her ring finger.

"You are sly, Mr.... Fitzwilliam. I did not know you had time to go to the jeweler's today."

Mr. Darcy gave her a small smile. "I am a man of many talents."

Elizabeth blushed, not from what he had said, but from his direct and warm gaze. She swallowed and straightened her dress. What did he mean by that?

Mr. Darcy cleared his throat. "It is customary for married couples to have a wedding night. However, since we did not have a courtship, I propose that we postpone our wedding night until we know each other better." Elizabeth released her breath and relaxed.

"I thank you, Mr.... Fitzwilliam. I much agree." She turned to him with a real smile.

Mr. Darcy returned her smile with a smaller one. "I do not wish the servants to gossip about our sleeping arrangements. I suggest we sleep in the same bed. However, I propose a scheme for us to become better acquainted."

Elizabeth bit her bottom lip and looked up at Mr. Darcy.

He paused and stared at her until he cleared his throat and continued. “I propose that we change for bed, then sit in bed and ask a question of each other. We do this every night until we feel we are properly knowledgeable about each other."

"I think it is a splendid idea."

Elizabeth walked behind the screen and changed into her nightclothes. She peeked around the screen to find her husband already sitting in bed. Head held up, she dashed to the bed, climbed in and pulled the covers up to her neck. She did not look at her husband at all. Elizabeth was sure her blush was as bright as a ripe tomato.

Mr. Darcy cleared his throat. "Who would you like to ask a question first?"

"I daresay you have just gone first, Fitzwilliam. You just asked a question." Elizabeth smiled and chanced a glance at her husband, who smiled back.

"Then it is your turn."

Elizabeth gave him a real smile. If Mr. Darcy could be playful, their marriage would soon be right as rain. "I would like to ask a question I asked earlier today.

How did your carriage come to be covered in so much snow?"

Mr. Darcy quirked his lips. "Mr. Bingley and I traveled to London yesterday to procure special licenses. The snowstorm caught us but could not stop our travel for fear we would not reach you in time. We had to stop as the driver could no longer see the road. We waited until the sun rose to finish our travel, and we arrived just in time."

It was such a thrilling tale. Mr. Darcy moved on the bed and brushed against Elizabeth. The touch sent a thrill up her side. "Why did you wait until the day before I was to be married to Mr. Collins to procure a special license?"

Elizabeth could not be sure, but it looked as if Mr. Darcy blushed.

"It took finding out about your upcoming wedding to Mr. Collins for me to realize the truth."

Elizabeth waited, but no more was forthcoming from Mr. Darcy. "And what truth was that?"

She had a small smile playing upon her lips as she glanced at Mr. Darcy.

He turned towards her. "That Mr. Collins was not worthy of you."

Elizabeth's face fell, and she turned to face forward. She had hoped to hear a declaration of some sort, that he had loved her since he first saw her. Did he even like her?

"It is my turn now to ask a question. If it does not bother you, I would like to know what happened to you at Longbourn. I overheard your uncle mention something today."

Elizabeth stared at her hands. The silence grew.

"I apologize for bringing up a subject that has troubled you." said Mr. Darcy.

"This is a troubling subject, and I would rather postpone our discussion of this matter to a later time."

"I am sorry for upsetting you. I will postpone the rest of my questions." Mr. Darcy leaned over to dim the lamp.

"No, please do not. I would like to learn more about you. I think your scheme of the questions is good. I would like to know your favorite pastime." Elizabeth tried not to bump into Mr. Darcy as he leaned back.

"I enjoy many things. To name a favorite would be difficult." Mr. Darcy paused. "I believe it would have to be reading a good book. What is yours?"

Elizabeth smiled. "It is also difficult for me. I would have to say reading a good book or taking a good walk. I love both dearly."

"I am glad to hear that. The library at Pemberley is large and the grounds have many walking paths through the gardens and woods."

Mr. Darcy looked devilishly handsome in this low light, or perhaps it was the fact that they were both in night clothes that had her heart beating so fast. "I cannot wait to see it. It sounds beautiful." Elizabeth turned her body towards Mr. Darcy. "What is your favorite part of Pemberley?"

Mr. Darcy leaned his head back to think. Elizabeth used the time to admire her husband's profile, and the muscled arms and chest that she could make out under his night shirt.

"There are so many things I love about Pemberley that it is difficult to settle on one. You ask maddening questions." Mr. Darcy turned his head and caught Elizabeth focused not on his countenance. He twitched his lips in a smile. He was gratified to see that his wife was not unaffected by his closeness. "I shall say the grounds of Pemberley. I love walking, fishing, riding, and being out in nature. Now it is my turn. What do you like most about this area you live in?"

Elizabeth looked up and blushed that she had been caught. "I believe that... I..." Elizabeth cleared her throat. "Pardon me. I enjoy the lack of populace. I would find living in a city to be confining and maddening. I love to be outside too much."

"I am glad to hear we are of like minds on that subject." Mr. Darcy smiled. Elizabeth was transfixed at how a smile changed his countenance. "I suggest we turn in."

Mr. Darcy bade Elizabeth a good night, and she did the same. It was awkward for both to share a bed with someone that was still a stranger. Elizabeth felt each movement Mr. Darcy made as he shifted on the bed. They each listened to the other breathe until Elizabeth fell asleep. Mr. Darcy stayed awake longer and wished he did not have such strong control over his emotions.

CHAPTER 24

The next morning arrived far too early. Elizabeth felt the bed move and was surprised Hill had not been in yet to open the curtains. Elizabeth opened her eyes and then opened them all the way as Mr. Darcy walked by in his nightshirt. She pinched her eyes closed and blushed. All the events of the day before came back to her. She was married to Mr. Darcy!

The image of Mr. Darcy in his nightshirt stayed in Elizabeth's mind. She wanted to bury herself under the covers, but feared that if she moved at all, Mr. Darcy would know she was awake and had seen him. So she stayed quiet. She heard noises that meant Mr.

Darcy was changing his clothes, which renewed her blush. This would never do. She could not walk around Netherfield in a continual blush when she was around Mr. Darcy.

He cleared his throat. "Elizabeth, are you by chance awake?"

He had caught her. "Yes, I am."

"I should like to wait for you so we may break our fast together. Would you like me to send a maid in?"

Elizabeth did not want servants to notice how shy was around Mr. Darcy. "No. I believe you can help me dress, if that would be amenable."

"Yes. I shall be across the room and face the wall until you call for me."

Elizabeth was sure she had not blushed as much as she had these last few days. Elizabeth opened her eyes to find Mr. Darcy turned around. She scampered out of the bed and behind the changing screen. In all the excitement and events of yesterday, she had not had time to think about what being a married woman entailed.

Elizabeth could not wait to talk to her friend Charlotte Lucas. She had so much to tell. Soon she was dressed except for the buttons in the back of her dress and her hair. Elizabeth walked out from behind the changing screen with her long hair draped over her shoulder. "Fitzwilliam, if you could button me up?"

Mr. Darcy turned and stared.

"I believe I need a maid to help me with my hair. Unless you are proficient with ladies hair styles?" Elizabeth teased Mr. Darcy.

A smile tugged at Mr. Darcy's lips. "Alas, no, I do not have that skill."

Mr. Darcy walked behind Elizabeth and buttoned up her dress. He then rang the bell, and a maid knocked on the door. She must have been standing in the hall waiting for a summons. The maid pinned Elizabeth's hair up, then Mr. Darcy and Elizabeth walked downstairs arm in arm.

They entered the dining room to find they were not the first to wake. Miss Bingley and Mrs. Hurst looked as if they had been interrupted in the middle of a conversation. They greeted each other, then Mr. Darcy prepared a plate for Elizabeth and one for himself.

Elizabeth liked this version of Mr. Darcy. Could it be possible that George Wickham had not been truthful regarding Mr. Darcy? She did not know what to think.

Elizabeth continued to smile while she ate. She looked up to find Miss Bingley scowling at her. Elizabeth did not change her expression nor look away. Miss Bingley excused herself and left the room. Elizabeth enjoyed her first morning at Netherfield.

~

ELIZABETH AND MR. DARCY walked on the grounds of Netherfield.

"I am glad you suggested a walk," said Elizabeth.

"As being out of doors is both our favorite pastime, I thought it was a good idea."

Elizabeth put her arms behind her back as she walked. She wanted to ask him about Wickham's stories but decided that should wait until they had been married longer, and when the danger of Mr. Darcy getting the marriage annulled had passed. She did not want to anger him so soon after their wedding.

"What were your favorite walks at Longbourn?"

Elizabeth smiled. "You are more talkative than when we last danced at the Netherfield Ball." She glanced at her husband.

"I certainly have not the talent which some people possess," said Darcy, "of conversing easily with those I do not know."

"I am glad to hear I am no longer in the category of stranger."

Mr. Darcy frowned at her. "I believe we are past strangers, Elizabeth."

Elizabeth blushed and glanced away. Her attempt at teasing Mr. Darcy did not go as planned. They walked in silence for several minutes, though it was not an uncomfortable silence.

"I fear we are back to searching for subjects to discuss." Conversing with Mr. Darcy had been easier in the dim light of their bedchamber last night. "Do you play a musical instrument?" Elizabeth glanced at her husband.

"I do not. That is not a skill I possess, though my younger sister is talented with the pianoforte."

"How do you occupy your time?"

"I am a man of leisure, but it does not mean I do not have obligations. There is the estate of Pemberley, the townhouse in London, the tenants, the fields and livestock, and my sister to attend to."

Elizabeth looked at him in surprise. "I apologize. I did not know. But your sister cannot give you much to attend to?" Elizabeth noticed Mr. Darcy's lips turned down, though he did not speak. Elizabeth did not question him as she could not judge him, as she had two sisters that gave her mother grief. "Will I see your sister soon? Is she at your house in town?"

"It is our house now, Elizabeth. And no, she is at Pemberley. She has a companion, Mrs. Annesley, and various masters that provide her lessons."

"She is not at a boarding school?"

Mr. Darcy shook his head. "After our father died, Georgiana was loath to be away from her only remaining family member. Truthfully, I felt the same. Now that I have educated her at home, neither one of us finds a boarding school amenable."

"Has she had a season in London?"

"No, as she is only five and ten."

"Oh, she is the same age as my youngest sister, Lydia. Though I imagine your sister Georgiana displays better behavior." Again Elizabeth noticed Mr. Darcy frown.

Their walk had circled back to the house. "If you do not mind," said Darcy, "I would like to ride my horse, Bucephalus."

"I do not mind. Thank you for accompanying me on a walk."

"Do you ride?"

Elizabeth shook her head. "Our horse was needed in the fields more often than not."

Mr. Darcy nodded and left for the stables. Elizabeth continued to walk as she was used to rambling a fair distance. She was determined to find a new path since her daily walk to Oakham Mount was no longer available to her.

After a while she heard horses. Soon she saw the militia ride by on their horses. She smiled at them and then waved when she saw George Wickham, who returned her greeting. Elizabeth found herself to be quite happy.

Elizabeth walked back into Netherfield, curious at the carriage in front. She removed her bonnet, and her smile fell when she heard her mother. She was visiting them so soon? Elizabeth walked into the sitting room to find Mrs. Bennet and all her sisters.

"Lizzy, you will not believe this! Mr. Collins has thrown us out!" Lydia exclaimed.

"And threw our trunks out in the snow," said Kitty, "and he would not let us in to get our things."

"We do not have even half of our clothing, not to mention our other things such as my parents' portraits! What shall we do?" Mrs. Bennet fluttered her handkerchief and wiped her eyes as she cried.

Elizabeth stared. "He would not let you in?"

"No indeed, he would not! We had to stay the night with my sister though it was very cramped. And without all our personal items! We have nowhere to stay." Mrs. Bennet cried.

Elizabeth turned and found Jane with an arm around Mary. "I am not surprised. These are not the actions of a gentleman."

Mr. Bingley entered the sitting room. "I have employed my steward to the task of finding a rental house for your family."

Mrs. Bennet raised her arms out to Mr. Bingley. "Oh Mr. Bingley, thank you! I do not know where we shall live until a rental house is found. We cannot stay at my sister's house again, it was much too small."

"Why can we not stay here? There are loads of enough rooms for all of us and I say half of Meryton too." Lydia twirled her hair around a finger.

Elizabeth looked upwards and then glanced at Jane who looked at Mr. Bingley and raised her eyebrows.

Mr. Bingley turned to Mrs. Bennet. "You can stay here, all of you, until a rental house is found."

"That is true gentlemanly behavior, unlike those who only look the part. Oh, why did Mr. Bennet die?" Mrs. Bennet cried again until Elizabeth and Jane escorted their mother upstairs to a bedchamber.

CHAPTER 25

That night, Mr. Darcy and Elizabeth continued their game of questions to know one another. Elizabeth was less embarrassed at being seen in her nightgown, though a thrill went up her spine every time Mr. Darcy looked at her.

"Who would you like to go first, Elizabeth?" Mr. Darcy looked at her.

Sitting so close in the bed, Elizabeth could feel the heat from his body. She licked her lips. "I believe I could go first tonight. Did you have a pet growing up?"

Mr. Darcy stared at her lips, then brought his eyes up to Elizabeth's. "Yes, I had several dogs as pets growing up. My favorite was a wolfhound I named Hercules."

Elizabeth smiled at the thought of a young Fitzwilliam playing. "And did he undertake the twelve labors of Hercules?"

Mr. Darcy beamed at Elizabeth. His visage was greatly improved with a smile. Elizabeth stared at his countenance. "He did. Every day he undertook the labors of Hercules. I miss him."

Elizabeth swallowed. "Do you have a favorite pet now?"

"I think my horse Bucephalus would be my favorite, though he is not a pet. I named him after Alexander the Great's horse."

"You seem to enjoy your history and mythology, Fitzwilliam." Elizabeth admired a man that knew his history and was well read. What luck that Mr. Darcy was her husband.

"I do. Now it is my turn. Did you have a pet as a child?"

"I did not. I played with our neighbors' piglets and chased them as a child. We had great fun trying to catch the greased pig." Elizabeth laughed, and Mr. Darcy joined her.

"I wish I could have seen that."

"We were a mess all covered with mud and torn dresses, but we had never had so much fun. I am not sure the piglet enjoyed it as much." They laughed again.

Mr. Darcy reached out for Elizabeth's hand and held it. She blushed at their touching while undressed, and also because she was growing to like Mr. Darcy.

THE NEXT DAY Elizabeth walked downstairs to find Mrs. Bennet and her youngest sisters dressed to leave. "My sister sent a note that she has news for us."

"I do hope we see some officers," Lydia exclaimed as they walked out the front door.

Elizabeth waved to them, then walked into the sitting room occupied by Mrs. Hurst, Miss Bingley, with Mary at the pianoforte. Elizabeth furrowed her brow and walked over to Mary. "You found your sheet music?"

Mary stopped her practice. "Mrs. Hurst has allowed me to learn her music though it requires greater skill than I possess."

Elizabeth leaned around to look at the sheet music and raised her eyebrows. That piece was the most complicated sheet music she had seen. Elizabeth smiled at Mary, then glanced at Mrs. Hurst who looked at them with a smirk. Could Mrs. Hurst even play that piece?

Elizabeth walked towards the seating arrangement and found a pile of books on an end table. She chose one that looked interesting and sat down to read. Several minutes passed in silence except for Mary trying to learn the new piece of music.

"And how is your family... Elizabeth?" Miss Bingley questioned. "Has a new rental house been found for them in Meryton?"

"I imagine Mr. Bingley's steward will find several that will suffice."

"And what of the estate? I have heard Mrs. Bennet tell that my brother will buy an estate for her." Miss Bingley and Mrs. Hurst exchanged looks.

Elizabeth blinked. "I have not heard that."

"Well let me assure you Elizabeth," said Miss. Bingley, "my brother will not buy your mother an estate." Miss Bingley and Mrs. Hurst giggled.

Elizabeth had never heard her mother state that Mr. Bingley would buy her an estate. She returned to her book and ignored the Bingley sisters. She would be happy if those two were far away. Perhaps Jane and Mr. Bingley could come to Pemberley with them when they left the area.

~

"Sister, sister you would not believe the news I have heard today!" Mrs. Phillips bade them enter.

"Oh yes? I could use a good distraction today. Mr. Bingley's steward has found us a rental house but it is still much too small."

"Franny, I have news for you of Longbourn."

Mrs. Bennet scowled at her sister. "Why do I care to hear of Longbourn? It is not my home anymore, thanks to that Mr. Collins. Did I not tell you that he threw our trunks in the snow? And without all our belongings! He would not let us in to get them."

Mrs. Phillips leaned closer. "That is what I want to tell you! Hill and the other servants have quit Longbourn. They will not work for him. They say he has a fierce temper."

Mrs. Bennet sat back in her chair with a smile. "Well, that should show him."

"But that is not all. The day of the weddings, Mr. Collins returned to Longbourn from the church in a high state. He smashed and threw all of your belongings and then had the servants burn them."

Mrs. Bennet gaped at her sister. "Burned them? But our clothing? All of our belongings?"

Lydia jumped up. "My bonnets! He did not destroy my bonnets, did he?"

"Or my dresses?" Kitty exclaimed.

"All of it. Vases smashed on the floor. Pictures taken off the wall and thrown at the floor. Glasses thrown in the fireplace. Clothing torn to shreds." Mrs. Phillips leaned back in her chair and nodded at her sister.

"This is outrageous! He had no right to destroy our possessions! Our brother said that everything we purchased after Mr. Bennet inherited Longbourn was ours. I was there when he told Mr. Collins." Mrs. Bennet stood. "I knew we needed the magistrate. Well, Mr. Collins will rue the day he crossed me!"

~

Miss Bingley gazed out a window at the carriage that had just arrived. She rolled her eyes then turned towards the sitting room. "Now, all of the ridiculous Bennets are here."

Elizabeth frowned. "Excuse me, Miss Bingley. I am not sure I heard you correctly. Could you repeat that?"

Miss Bingley walked to her sister and sat down. "I merely stated that the Bennet carriage had arrived."

Miss Bingley smiled serenely at Elizabeth, who flattened her lips. Since Mr. Bingley and Mr. Darcy were in the game room, Miss Bingley must have thought she could insult the Bennets without censure.

Mrs. Bennet entered the sitting room at a brisk walk. "I have just heard the most distressing news about that odious Mr. Collins. You will not believe what I heard." Mrs. Bennet sat in an armchair. "Hill and all the servants have quit Longbourn! Not only that, but Hill told Mrs. Phillips that Mr. Collins had all our belongings burned! There is not a thread left of clothing, paintings or anything." Mrs. Bennet leaned back. "I am sure Hill exaggerated for dramatic effect, but nonetheless, we need the magistrate!"

Elizabeth glanced at the Bingley sisters and saw them share a long look. Elizabeth looked back at Mrs. Bennet. "I am sure Mr. Collins would not have destroyed or burned our belongings. Perhaps he will be more amenable to our request to gather our belongings now that the servants have left."

"He will be lucky indeed if he can get anyone else to work for him after word of his behavior spreads through the county." Mrs. Bennet pursed her lips. "We need the help of the magistrate!"

Mr. Darcy and Mr. Bingley entered the room having finished their game of billiards. They greeted the Bennets and then walked over to their respective wives.

Mr. Bingley kissed Jane on the cheek. "What was this I heard you say about the magistrate, Mrs. Bennet?"

"It is time for the magistrate to question Mr. Collins regarding our belongings. It is an embarrassment that he should treat his own relations in this manner!"

Elizabeth felt Mr. Darcy's hand on her shoulder. "I believe Mr. Bingley and I can assist in this matter. We will visit the magistrate and bring him to Longbourn."

"Oh, what marvelous sons you are. I have the best son-in-laws in all of Hertfordshire. Let us do this at once. If I hear another word from Lydia about her bonnets---"

"But Mama, my bonnets! I worked hard on them. Even Susan Miller said they were well done," said Lydia.

~

Elizabeth dressed for bed and sat under the covers while Mr. Darcy changed. Her mind was full of the news Mrs. Bennet had shared from Mrs. Phillips, that the servants said Mr. Collins had them destroy the Bennet's belongings. She looked down at her hands on the bed covers. Elizabeth found it hard to believe Mr. Collins would be so mean and destructive but she did not doubt the servant's word.

She was grateful to Mr. Darcy for her rescue from that man. Though she did not like Mr. Darcy's actions towards George Wickham, her first impression of him had changed because of his actions towards her. Plus, he married her, and she was determined to not cause Mr. Darcy to seek an annulment.

Mr. Darcy climbed into bed and sat next to Elizabeth. She felt him brush the side of her leg which sent a thrill and warmth through her body. She adjusted her position in bed and brushed her shoulder against his. Elizabeth flushed and again felt a thrill travel through her body. She wanted to scoot away, so she did not keep touching him but she also did not want to insult him. So she stayed where she sat. Had Mr. Darcy sat closer to her than he had the night before?

"I am sorry for the loss of your belongings, Elizabeth. Were there any possessions still at Longbourn that you will miss?"

Elizabeth glanced over to him then widened her eyes as she saw Mr. Darcy was closer than he had been last night. "I had nothing valuable. What I cherished

I had already brought here with me such as books and a few necklaces. But what I could not get was a memento of my father. I hope Mr. Collins has not destroyed everything in my father's study."

"I apologize for asking a question that brought you discomfort."

Elizabeth looked at her hands. She could not believe this was the same man that acted so proud and arrogant. Mr. Darcy had greatly improved since then. "When did you realize you were interested in offering for me?"

Mr. Darcy shifted. "I did not realize how much you fascinated me until I noticed you occupied my thoughts often. Your easy nature, laughter, and quick mind captivated me. I realized no other woman had never fascinated me as you had."

Elizabeth smiled and felt a thrill at Mr. Darcy's confession. She glanced up at him to find his gaze upon her. She blushed but did not look away. He had a smile on his lips. Mr. Darcy was handsome and at this close distance, he overwhelmed her. Elizabeth blushed and looked away.

Mr. Darcy cleared his throat. "I think we should retire for the night." He blew out his candle.

Elizabeth did the same to hers and scooted under the covers. She laid on her back and stared up at the ceiling. She felt Mr. Darcy move on his side of the bed. His arm brushed hers and a thrill shot through her. She rolled her lips and wished she could be so bold as to hold his hand. But, she did not want him to think she was a light-skirt. Perhaps, it was best to do nothing. Elizabeth fell asleep as she wished she could hold Mr. Darcy's hand.

CHAPTER 26

The next day, Mr. Darcy and Mr. Bingley visited the magistrate, who was all too happy to do whatever was needed for the illustrious Mr. Darcy and his wealthy friend Mr. Bingley. And so it was three carriages that arrived at Longbourn.

The magistrate knocked upon the front door and waited. He knocked again and Mr. Collins opened the door. He wore wrinkled clothes, his hair was not combed, and it did not look like he had kept up with his hygiene. The party shared looks of disgust.

"Mr. Collins, the Bennet family needs to collect their belongings."

Mr. Collins smiled and nodded to the party. "Do come in. My servants already packed everything for them, as that was the least I could do for my cousins, but if they feel they are missing something they are free to look around."

The magistrate led the way into Longbourn followed by Mrs. Bennet, Mr. Bingley with Jane, Mr. Darcy with Elizabeth, and the rest of the Bennets. Elizabeth was uncomfortable to be near Mr. Collins. She walked down the hall and turned into the sitting room.

Elizabeth gasped. "The room is nearly empty!"

Jane and Mr. Bingley had followed them into the sitting room. Jane covered her mouth. "I wonder if the rest of the house is this empty," Jane whispered to Elizabeth. "Perhaps Hill did not exaggerate and Mr. Collins destroyed everything that belonged to us."

Elizabeth reached out and squeezed Jane's hand. "I want to go to Papa's study. I want a memento of him if there is anything left."

"I will accompany you." Mr. Darcy cocked his arm, and they exited the sitting room.

Elizabeth turned the handle for the study, but the door was locked.

Mr. Darcy walked back into the hallway. "Mr. Collins, if you could open the study. My wife would like a memento of her father."

"Oh yes, Mr. Darcy." Mr. Collins bowed then walked down the hall and opened the study.

Elizabeth's gasp was louder this time. "It is all gone. The books, statues, wall hangings. They are all gone!"

"My cousin Elizabeth, I do not understand what you mean. This room is as it was when you left it."

Elizabeth stared.

Mr. Darcy focused on Mr. Collins. "What do you mean by that statement *after she left it?* Explain yourself."

"Mr. Darcy, you are angry at the wrong person here. Why, after I came back from the wedding I found the house just like this."

"Are you stating that someone robbed you while you were at the church?"

"Indeed, Mr. Darcy. When I came back from the church, I found the house like this. The Bennet girls had obviously come back and taken their things."

Elizabeth pursed her lips. "And how were we to have done that, Mr. Collins? We were at the church. You left before any of us did."

"One does not have to be present to take things away from a house."

Mr. Darcy stepped closer to Mr. Collins. "Be careful of what you are implying, Mr. Collins. My wife is no thief. These items of her father's belonged to the Bennets. They were personal effects of the late Mr. Bennet."

Mr. Collins backed out of the room into the hall. "I apologize, Mr. Darcy." Mr. Collins nodded and walked away.

Mr. Darcy turned back to Elizabeth, who stood scowling. "Elizabeth, let us see if someone has moved the items."

"I am sure now that what Hill told Aunt Phillips is true. He destroyed everything and burned it. Let us go to the back of the house and check if there has been a recent fire."

Elizabeth and Mr. Darcy walked out the back door to find a large area with no snow, only ash. "We will tell the magistrate of this. I am sorry for what happened to your father's belongings."

Elizabeth took a deep breath and gave her husband a smile. "Thank you. I cannot believe Mr. Collins destroyed it all. He took that away from us."

Mr. Darcy took Elizabeth's hand. "Mr. Collins can never destroy your memories of your father, though."

The couple walked back into the house to inform the magistrate of their findings. They heard exclamations as the rest of the family discovered the bare rooms upstairs.

"My bonnets are all gone? Why would Mr. Collins get rid of my bonnets?"

"The portraitures of my parents are missing!" Mrs. Bennet stormed down the steps to where Mr. Collins stood in the entryway with a serene smile. "Mr. Collins, tell me what you have done with our belongings?"

Mr. Darcy stepped forward. "I believe the story Mr. Collins told us was that someone robbed him while we were at church."

The magistrate turned to Mr. Collins. "Robbed, do you say? Why did you not contact me? You have never said a word of this, though I have seen you several times in Meryton."

"I did not want to scare the fine residents of Meryton with the knowledge that there was a thief amongst them."

Mr. Darcy heard Elizabeth take a breath, and he squeezed her arm. "There is also a burned area in the back," said Mr. Darcy. “It was made after the fresh snow that fell Saturday morning."

The magistrate turned to Mr. Collins. "A large burn area? And what did you need to burn after Saturday morning, Mr. Collins?"

"I do none of the work here. As you know, I am the owner of Longbourn. The servants do the cooking, the cleaning and everything else. I do not know what they do. I am sure if you question them, they could tell you they were doing some chore."

The magistrate narrowed his eyes. "And, where are your servants, Mr. Collins? I have not seen one since we have arrived."

"I believe they must be---"

"You fired Hill and the other servants, Mr. Collins." Mrs. Bennet exclaimed. "My sister told me so when she spoke with Hill today."

"I need to speak to the servants to find out what happened here." The magistrate frowned at Mr. Collins. "If there has been a robbery, there will have to be an inquiry as to the Bennets' claim that their belongings are missing."

Mrs. Bennet spoke, "There was no robbery by thieves, only the robbery Mr. Collins committed! Hill, a servant that worked for us at Longbourn for years, told my sister, Mrs. Phillips, that Mr. Collins destroyed all of our belongings! He threw them to the floor, smashed them, tore our clothing and had it all burned!"

The magistrate turned to address Mr. Collins. "This is a serious accusation by Mrs. Bennet. Destruction of property is theft, which is a hanging offense. What do you have to say for yourself?"

Mr. Collins wiped sweat off his brow. "I do not know what Mrs. Bennet means. You would take the word of a servant, heresay, gossip, over the word of a man of the cloth?"

The magistrate frowned at Mr. Collins, then turned to Mr. Darcy. "I apologize for this, sir. I shall open an inquiry. I will question the servants if someone could provide me with their names and places of living."

Mr. Darcy nodded and then led Elizabeth out of Longbourn. The rest of the Bennet family followed with Mrs. Bennet and Lydia voicing their displeasure at their missing belongings. Tears ran down Mary's visage. She had spent years compiling her library of music.

Elizabeth and Darcy changed for bed as they had every night before.

"Are you ready with your question for tonight, Elizabeth?"

Elizabeth was not ready, and indeed she had forgotten Mr. Darcy's idea to ask questions. "I apologize, Fitzwilliam. I do not have a question ready. It does not mean I do not place importance upon this nor do not value this, as I do. It is that the events of the day are foremost in my mind."

"I understand. I am sorry that Mr. Collins has behaved so abominably toward your family."

"Thank you. Mary is upset over the loss of her sheet music. She had saved her pin money for years and had a collection of pieces."

Mr. Darcy turned to Elizabeth. "She may order what she wants, and I will pay for them."

Elizabeth smiled. "You may regret offering that, but thank you. That is very generous of you."

Mr. Darcy turned to Elizabeth. "It is no bother. It matters to Mary and therefore to you."

Elizabeth smiled. Then turned to look back down at her hands. She could not make out her husband's character. She had her own experiences to draw upon, but they differed greatly from before their wedding and after. Also, there were George Wickham's accounts of Darcy's treatment. Which one was the real Mr. Darcy? She did not know. She wished to ask Mr. Darcy about Wickham's stories soon, however she would wait until she felt more secure in her marriage.

Mr. Darcy did not ask his questions of Elizabeth as he felt it would not be fair since she did not have any.

They bade each other good night and lay down to sleep. Elizabeth was still getting used to sleeping with a man in the bed. She held herself still so she would not accidentally brush against him, no matter how much she secretly wished to do so. She felt a thrill every time that happened. Despite her thoughts, she fell asleep sooner than she had the other nights.

CHAPTER 27

The next day, Mrs. Bennet and the youngest Bennets left with Mr. Bingley's steward again to view the rental houses that were available in Meryton.

Lydia and Kitty exited the rental house and waved to Denny, who walked with other members of the militia across the street. "Denny! Denny!"

"Come on, let us go to Denny." The two youngest Bennet girls ran across the street to the officers, ignoring proper decorum for their mourning period. They found the officers much too enticing.

"Now that we will live in Meryton, we can see you every day." Lydia hung onto Denny's arm.

"It is our pleasure," said Denny.

"I heard the Longs are having a card party tonight. I wish we could go, but we are in mourning. I will miss you all. You too, Wickham." Lydia smiled at the group of men in their uniforms that surrounded her.

Wickham nodded to Lydia. "Indeed, you will be missed most of all."

Lydia tilted her head. "I cannot wait to play lottery tickets again. Why does our mourning have to last so long? I bet I could get more tickets than all of you. I wonder what prizes the Longs will have?"

The group began a lively discussion of their favorite card games and prizes. Wickham touched Lydia's arm and pulled her back from the group. Lydia said nothing at the want of propriety.

"How are you faring these days, Miss Bennet?"

"Oh, I am doing quite well." Lydia fluttered her eyelashes.

"Have you heard from your sister, Elizabeth? How does she find Netherfield?"

Lydia frowned. "They will not let us live there. It is not fair!“

"I saw your sister walk far from Netherfield today. Does she often go on long walks?"

"She walks all the time, and not even to visit friends! I find it boring. If she would walk to Meryton or the Lucas' I would go with her but now that---"

"Does she find the morning better for her walks? Is there a certain time of day that she enjoys a walk more than others?"

"I do not know why you are asking about Elizabeth. She is already married. There are many girls not yet married and still unattached." Lydia tilted her head and smiled.

The sudden absence of the normal sounds of the street had both Wickham and Lydia turn. Mr. Collins walked in front of the shops as he nodded and smiled. Many crossed the street or looked away.

"There is Mr. Collins now! I cannot believe Mama would force me to marry him."

"Indeed?" Wickham looked at Lydia.

"Oh yes, but Mr. Barrow refused to marry us since I said that I would not. Who would want to marry that vile man?" Lydia continued to scowl at Mr. Collins back.

Wickham bowed to Lydia. "I must take my leave now and return to the barracks. A soldier's work is never done." He joined the other soldiers as they continued their walk in Meryton.

Lydia waved then joined Kitty with laughter as they compared who they thought were the most handsome. Mrs. Bennet and Mr. Bingley's steward exited the rental house.

~

WHEN SUPPER WAS FINALLY over that night, the women left for the sitting room. Mary sat down at the pianoforte and continued to struggle with the difficult piece of music that Mrs. Hurst had lent her.

"Mama, when will we have to move into our rental home? I do not see why we cannot stay here," Lydia said to the censure of her older sisters.

"We cannot stay at Netherfield as it is your sister's home. I need my own house to be mistress of and I would like to be closer to my sister in Meryton. We shall move tomorrow, but we can always visit my married daughters." Mrs. Bennet beamed at Jane and Elizabeth. Elizabeth smiled and made a point to not look at the Bingley sisters.

Lydia and Kitty held a whispered conversation and then left the sitting room to run down the hallway to the game room. Elizabeth closed her eyes. Her family's move to Meryton could not come soon enough.

Mary quit her practice of the pianoforte not long after and came to sit next to Elizabeth. Elizabeth looked up from her book and squeezed Mary's hand. "I am sure you will get your sheet music soon. I will ask Mr. Darcy---"

Mrs. Hurst interrupted Elizabeth by playing the same difficult piece with exquisite skill and speed. Elizabeth could not finish the discussion with Mary, and instead they sat while Mrs. Hurst displayed her proficiency. Mrs. Hurst finished with a flourish and smiled at the Bennet sisters.

"That was so well done, Louisa," Miss Bingley congratulated her sister. "I am astonished at how well you play that instrument. How proud I am of your skill."

Mary stiffened. "Pride is a very common failing, I believe. By all that I have ever read, I am convinced that it is very common indeed that human nature is particularly prone to it. There are very few of us who do not cherish the feeling of self-complacency on the score of some quality or other, real or imaginary. Vanity and pride are different things though the words are often used synonymously. A person may be proud without being vain."

Elizabeth hid her smile under her hand as Mary rose and left the room.

~

Elizabeth changed into her nightgown as she hummed. The floor was cold, so she stood on the rug and leaned over to open her trunk as she looked for the handmade book that Mary had made for her birthday. Elizabeth had always thought she would do grand things with the book like drawings of nature, poetry or even little paintings. But, art was not her forte. She had finally used it to press a flower from that summer.

But now Elizabeth had decided she would use the book to record events of her new married life. She would start the diary when she first married Mr. Darcy. Or even before that, when her father died because that started everything that came after.

Elizabeth sat down at the little writing desk in the room's corner. She wrote her name and date on the first page.

Mr. Darcy entered the room and walked over to Elizabeth. "You are writing a letter?"

Elizabeth smiled at his confusion. "No, this is a blank book that Mary made for me and gave on my birthday. I had not used it except to press a flower. But now I shall use it to record the memorable moments since I have started my new life as your wife."

"That was a nice gift. She has skill with binding books. Perhaps I shall hire her to rebind the books in my library at Pemberley."

Elizabeth stared at her husband. She did not know her husband well enough to determine whether he was teasing. "That is admirable of you. However, I am not sure how much---"

"Pardon me Elizabeth, I was teasing you. It is true books in my library at Pemberley need rebinding but

I would never state that your family needed to earn their way. No, I meant---"

Elizabeth had to save Mr. Darcy from his awkward apology. "Oh Fitzwilliam, no apology is necessary."

Mr. Darcy nodded to her. "I will do better in the future to make it known when I am making a joke."

Elizabeth looked sharply at him and saw the corners of his lip curled up along with a twinkle in his eye. She relaxed her shoulders. "Fitzwilliam, you are very sly."

At that he smiled. "I shall leave you to your note taking while I change my attire for bed."

Elizabeth turned back to her book, but it was difficult to concentrate while she listened to the sounds of Fitzwilliam's clothes being removed. She did not realize how distracted she had been until she read her note that was not about her wedding but instead stated *he is changing his clothes and he is naked in the room with me.*

Elizabeth set the quill down and covered her face with her hands. Thank goodness no one would read this except for her. Elizabeth blotted the page and closed her book. She climbed into bed soon followed by Mr. Darcy.

"Who shall go first tonight?"

Elizabeth kept her face on her hands as she was not sure she would not laugh and confess what she had just wrote in her book. "I think you should."

That would give her more time to compose herself. Besides, she did not have a question in mind to ask.

"What is your most favorite memory?"

That was not the type of question she had been expecting. "I have so many happy memories of rambling around Longbourn. I would have to say my walks when I found a bird's nest with baby birds, deer with fawns, having a butterfly land on me or finding a shiny rock. Those are some of my favorite memories."

Elizabeth turned to Mr. Darcy. "What is your most favorite memory?"

"I think it is when I was a boy and my father taught me how to fish. I was surprised when I felt my line pull. My father helped me pull the line in and we found a big trout on the end. I could not believe I had caught that myself. I remember staring at the pond amazed that fish had been in the water and I had caught it. I had it that night for dinner. That was a big day for me." Mr. Darcy turned to Elizabeth with a smile.

"I am glad to hear you are skilled in fishing. If ever we need our stores of food restocked, we can count on you. Do you hunt too?"

"You jest, madam. I hunt and bring down a good number of fowl and deer."

"We shall never go hungry then." Elizabeth's lips twitched, but she did not want to make Mr. Darcy feel she was laughing at him.

"I will always take care of you, Elizabeth. I do not plan to drive Pemberley to ruin and be forced to fish and hunt to provide for us."

Elizabeth flushed, embarrassed that Mr. Darcy had misunderstood her teasing. She reached across them and touched Mr. Darcy's arm. "Fitzwilliam, I was teasing you. I did not mean to make light of your skills or your commitment to Pemberley. I apologize."

Mr. Darcy held Elizabeth's hand. "It seems we still have more to learn about each other. I apologize for not knowing you were joking."

Elizabeth laughed. "We shall have to give a signal to each other when we are about to tease or make a joke. Perhaps a wink or we touch our nose so that there are no more misunderstandings?"

"If you make sure to look at me with a twinkle in your eye, I believe I may be able to catch when you are joking, ma'am."

Elizabeth saw the twinkle in Mr. Darcy's eye. She squeezed his hand. "And, I know you are joking because of the twinkle in your eye."

A large smile formed on Mr. Darcy's countenance. "You are correct. What would you like to claim as your prize for guessing correctly?"

Elizabeth felt a thrill of run through her. "I should like a kiss, sir."

Mr. Darcy's eyebrows rose, and he looked at her lips. Heat shot through her and then she closed her eyes as Mr. Darcy leaned in. She felt the pressure of his lips, smelled the scent of him, felt the warmth of his body. He pulled back and Elizabeth opened her eyes.

Mr. Darcy cleared his throat. "I think that is enough for tonight." He leaned over and blew out the candle.

Elizabeth's smile fell as she had hoped for she knew not what, but just... more. She leaned over and blew out her candle then scooted down in bed and pulled the covers up.

Elizabeth closed her eyes and tried to go to sleep but her thoughts were full of any movement that Mr. Darcy made. She could not focus on anything but him. Elizabeth had been glad when he suggested that they postpone the wedding night to know each other first, but now she was not sure it would not drive her mad in the meantime. She wanted to touch him, for him to hold her, to kiss her. However, she did not want him to think of her as a harlot, so she laid still and somehow fell asleep.

CHAPTER 28

The next day proved to be one of those beautiful winter days perfect for walking. In the dining room Elizabeth professed her plans. "It looks to be a nice day out today. I plan to go on one of my walks. Would you care to join me, Mr. Darcy?"

Mr. Darcy turned to Elizabeth. "I have important business I need to attend to first, but I will catch up to you on horseback when I am done. Is there a particular area you will walk today?"

"Mrs. Darcy is such a prodigious walker. She walks all over, not letting dirt or mud on her petticoats stop her." Miss Bingley smiled at Elizabeth.

"Oh yes, Elizabeth likes to walk. I have always told her she walked too much that no man would want a wife that walked instead of doing embroidery but well..." Mrs. Bennet looked down and fussed with her napkin.

Elizabeth looked heavenwards and flattened her lips. Her mother and younger sisters would be gone from Netherfield soon; she just had to get through this meal.

Mr. Darcy addressed Miss Bingley. "I find that exercise improves one's self, much the same as reading a book does for one's mind."

Elizabeth smiled as Mr. Darcy turned back to her. "Where might I find you when I am done with my business?"

"I believe I shall walk west again today. I should like to find a path that leads to Meryton."

"Then, you shall be able to walk to visit us at our new house in Meryton!" said Lydia, who forgot that they were still in their period of mourning for Mr. Bennet's death.

Elizabeth loved to walk in all seasons but there was something magical about a walk in the winter. The snow on the ground left a silence over the surroundings as if you were the only one present in this winter wonderland. Elizabeth walked west as her goal was to find the path her family used when they walked to Meryton from Longbourn.

She suddenly shivered and stopped. Elizabeth crossed her arms in front of her chest and turned in a circle. She could see no one, heard nothing out of the ordinary but she had an odd feeling she was being watched. She shook her head. "Do not be a goosecap, Elizabeth."

She continued her walk down the same path she had been taking every day since she moved into Netherfield. She had walked some distance when she heard twigs snap and a noise.

Elizabeth stopped and stood still, sure a stag was to appear. She loved watching the large creatures. If she stood still, they would leave her alone and not run off right away allowing her to view them.

The noise turned out to be rhythmic and sounded like someone was walking the same path she was on. Perhaps it was Charlotte Lucas? Elizabeth smiled at seeing her friend again, but it was not a majestic deer or Charlotte that strolled into view. It was Mr. Collins.

He stopped when he saw Elizabeth. His countenance was red from the weather or exertion. "My cousin Elizabeth, I did not expect to find you walking back to Longbourn so soon."

Elizabeth pursed her lips. "I am out for a walk, Mr. Collins. I am not heading towards Longbourn."

"But you are on my land now." Mr. Collins held the edge of his jacket and tilted his head.

Elizabeth looked around but saw nothing familiar to Longbourn's grounds. "I do not believe this is your land, Mr. Collins. I have walked all over Longbourn and I do not recognize this being part of it." Elizabeth gave a perfunctory curtsy and walked past Mr. Collins, but he grabbed her arm. Elizabeth was alarmed at his boorish behavior. Mr. Collins was a stickler for following society's rules. Why did he not follow them now?

"Do not deny that you have come here to beg for forgiveness." Mr. Collins' small eyes narrowed as he focused on Elizabeth.

She gaped at Mr. Collins. "Beg for forgiveness?" Elizabeth pulled her arm. "Unhand me!" She pulled her arm again. "Mr. Collins, it is you who should beg for forgiveness from us. You have destroyed my family's belongings at Longbourn and told a lie to the magistrate that someone robbed you! Now, unhand me at once. It is not proper that you hold on to me!"

Elizabeth swallowed and struggled more to free herself. Something was not right with this situation. She tried to suppress her fear, but it was difficult as Mr. Collins acted increasingly more strange.

"This is all your fault. If you had married me, none of this would have happened. Your mother told me you were an obstinate girl, but I did not believe her. I should have listened to her and not offered for you at all, but once I had, I could not take it back." With each of the statements, Mr. Collins stressed his feelings by shaking Elizabeth's arm.

"Mr. Collins, let go of me!" Elizabeth could not back away as his hold on her arm was too tight. She was now quite frightened and concerned as to what Mr. Collins would do to her.

He stepped closer to Elizabeth. "You are an ungrateful, willful child and should have been disciplined ages ago. If you were my wife, I would have seen to it directly. Now, I have no wife, and you have brought the magistrate down upon me. You owe me!" He grabbed both her arms and shook Elizabeth.

"Mr. Collins, you are delusional! It is the right of every woman to change her mind. And, you received Longbourn per the entailment. We do not owe you anything. Now, unhand me!" Elizabeth pulled and twisted but could not dislodge Mr. Collins grip on her arms. She then kicked at his legs.

"You should never have married someone so far above you, as Mr. Darcy. He is the nephew of my patroness, Lady Catherine de Bourgh!"

Mr. Collins pulled her so close to him that she could smell his horrible breath. Elizabeth turned her head away. She could no longer kick at him either as he was too close to her. Oh, that he would get done blathering and let her go! Was that horse hoofbeats she heard?

"She is most displeased with her nephew and you for ensnaring him with your charms and feminine wiles. You have damaged my standing with her, as it was my cousin who married the illustrious Mr. Darcy! You, who do not have the proper standing to be married into that family!" Mr. Collins shook Elizabeth with each accusation. The sleeve of her jacket ripped.

"Mr. Collins! How dare you---" Elizabeth turned her head back to yell at Mr. Collins though she was brought up short by his terrifying visage.

"You should have learned to keep your mouth shut and obey your betters!" Mr. Collins released an arm and smacked her across the face.

CHAPTER 29

Mr. Darcy finished his last letter, which was to his steward at Pemberley. He sealed the letter with wax and his signet ring, then stood and stretched. Now, he could enjoy riding outdoors in the company of his beautiful wife. He vowed to introduce her to the joys of horse riding that day, by having her ride Bucephalus at a walk back to Netherfield. He would walk next to her and they could continue to talk and learn about each other. Mr. Darcy smiled at the idea.

Mr. Darcy mounted Bucephalus and rode in the direction that Elizabeth indicated she would walk that day. He admired Elizabeth's dedication to going outside daily for walks, though he would much rather be on horseback. Mr. Darcy slowed his horse as he searched for the path to Meryton. He did not want to canter and overtake Elizabeth or come upon her too quickly and startle her.

With the horse making less noise at a trot, Mr. Darcy heard screams. He turned his head to determine their direction and urged Bucephalus into a canter.

Elizabeth heard horse's hoofbeats come closer. She hoped someone would hear her and stop to get Mr. Collins off of her. "Help me! Help!"

She was scared that he would succeed and ravage her before she had even had a wedding night with her own husband, Mr. Darcy.

Mr. Darcy followed the screams through a patch of trees into a small meadow. He pulled back on his horse before they ran down Mr. Collins struggling with Elizabeth.

"Help me with this termagant, Wickham! You said it would be easy to overtake her!" Mr. Collins struggled with greater fervor.

"Unhand her at once!" Mr. Darcy jumped off his horse.

Mr. Collins turned back and blanched at the sight of Mr. Darcy. Elizabeth pushed him off of her and rolled away. Mr. Collins was frozen in place on his hands and knees, unable to move. He just watched Mr. Darcy run closer.

Mr. Darcy dropped his riding crop, pulled Mr. Collins up and punched him in the face. "You worthless scum! How dare you call yourself a man of the cloth! I have a mind to beat you to a pulp!"

Elizabeth ran to Mr. Darcy, held onto his back and shivered. She cowered behind his wide back ashamed at her fear and yet terrified at what had almost happened. She could not believe what Mr. Collins had cried out, that he expected Wickham! And that Wickham said she would be easy to overtake?

Mr. Darcy turned and held Elizabeth by her arms, but she gasped in pain, which caused him to let go. "Elizabeth! I.."

Mr. Darcy looked Elizabeth over with his hands out wanting to hold her, to ease her fear but scared to touch her because she was in pain.

Elizabeth's jacket was torn, her bonnet hung by the ribbons, her dress was twisted and dirty. "Oh, Mr. Darcy!" Then Elizabeth burst into tears.

"May I hold you?" Mr. Darcy knew he should check that Mr. Collins was still on the ground but his wife needed him. He would console her quickly and then tie up Mr. Collins.

Elizabeth nodded. "Yes, please hold me. But be careful as my arms hurt from where he held me. Oh, Fitzwilliam!"

Mr. Darcy held Elizabeth as she cried. He had heard Elizabeth yell for help but was sure Mr. Collins had yelled something before Mr. Darcy dismounted. What was it?

"Did he... are you..." Mr. Darcy cleared his throat. "I must get you to Mr. Jones so he can check you."

Elizabeth shook her head. "He did not... ravage me. But he held my arms and they hurt. My jacket is torn."

Mr. Darcy held her, too scared to hold her tightly in case he caused more pain. Then, he saw the right side of her face was swelling. "Did he hit you on your face as well?"

Elizabeth nodded against his chest.

Mr. Darcy ground his teeth. He would gladly beat Mr. Collins and leave him for dead but he needed to get Elizabeth home. Damn that Mr. Collins! He needed to check on him, to make sure he was still down.

"I cannot believe he attacked me. And he yelled out thinking you were Mr. Wickham! He said that Wickham had said I would be easy to overpower!" Elizabeth leaned back and looked up at Mr. Darcy who blanched with widened eyes.

"Mr. Wickham?"

Elizabeth nodded her head.

Mr. Darcy scowled, let go of Elizabeth and picked up his riding crop from where he had tossed it. He turned towards Mr. Collins and stilled.

Elizabeth also turned to Mr. Collins and gasped.

"No, you will go nowhere," said Mr. Collins who held a pistol trained on the pair. "You owe me a wife." Mr. Collins tilted his head.

"I am sorry you have been taken in by my cousin Elizabeth. You are much too good for her, Mr. Darcy.

My patroness, Lady Catherine de Bourgh, talks often of how proud she is of you, Mr. Darcy." Mr. Collins seemed to start a bow and then stand up straight.

"I hate to do this, as you are the nephew of my patroness, who I hold in much esteem. But, you have made me the laughingstock of Meryton. And, your aunt is most displeased with your marriage. You were supposed to marry your cousin, Anne de Bourgh." Mr. Collins shook his head, almost as if it was a tic.

"I have been made a laughingstock when my patroness has told me to marry well and live in Longbourn. I cannot do that now and it is all your fault." Mr. Collins bowed his head again though at an angle. "I have displeased my patroness."

Elizabeth looked again at the pistol Mr. Collins held and gaped. "Is that not my father's pistol from his study?"

"No, it is my pistol. Everything in Longbourn belongs to me. And I will have what was supposed to be mine. You should not have sullied yourself Mr. Darcy with a woman so far below your standing." Mr. Collins walked towards the pair with an arm outstretched towards Elizabeth.

Elizabeth backed away from Mr. Collins while still holding on to Mr. Darcy. She stopped and tilted her head as she heard hoofbeats. Was it Mr. Wickham who Mr. Collins expected, or someone else that could help save them?

"Mr. Collins, think. My aunt holds you in esteem, which is why she granted you the living at Hunsford parsonage. I do not think Lady Catherine de Bourgh would be pleased if you shot me." Mr. Darcy stood still and watched Mr. Collins' hand upon the pistol.

"She is not pleased with you, Mr. Darcy. No, she is not pleased at all. She is quite angry. Her letter was most shocking. I do not think she would mind if you were given a beating. Because of your choice of wife, she would think getting shot would be a lesson as to the dangers of not doing what you were told for the betterment of your family. I am forever my patroness' obedient servant in all she commands." Mr. Collins stepped closer.

Mr. Darcy lashed out with his riding crop. He hoped to distract Mr. Collins, but did better and scored a direct hit across his face.

CHAPTER 30

Mr. Collins screamed, dropped the pistol and held his hands to his face. He tripped and fell backwards screaming. "My face! My eye! You hit my eye!"

Now that Mr. Collins was incapacitated, and in considerable pain, Mr. Darcy turned to his wife. "We must hurry as I heard hoofbeats. You must get on Bucephalus and then---"

Mr. Darcy turned away towards his mount but a horse walked out of the woods to block their path. On the horse was none other than George Wickham with a pistol in his hand.

Elizabeth gasped and stood behind Mr. Darcy. This was too much. She had thought Wickham her friend! She could not believe what Mr. Collins had said earlier about Wickham being expected. But now that Wickham was here, and holding a pistol on her and Mr. Darcy, she had to face the reality that Wickham was not the gentleman he made himself out to be. Even his tales about Mr. Darcy were probably lies!

George Wickham in his regimentals, smiled. "I do so enjoy shocking you, Fitzwilliam. Step away from her or I will gladly shoot you. As a matter of fact, I might shoot you first."

Elizabeth shivered. Tears formed and rolled down her face. She held onto the back of Mr. Darcy's jacket and hid behind his form.

"Wickham, throw down your pistol! There is no need to take out your hatred of me on Elizabeth."

Wickham still smiled and did not move his pistol. "Have you told Elizabeth about me yet? How we were best friends as children until you turned on me?" Wickham looked at Elizabeth. "He will throw you away Elizabeth, like he does with all his friends. You will fare no better. Come and I will save you from him."

"Leave her alone, Wickham! She has done nothing to you! Let her leave!" Mr. Darcy held his arms away from his sides as he slowly walked backwards and to the right, towards his horse.

"Oh, but I cannot, Fitzwilliam for she has done something to me. She has captured my interest. I will not let her go until I have a sample of her charming self."

Elizabeth held on tighter to Mr. Darcy's coat. This was a nightmare! And to think at one time she fancied Wickham? Was no one as they seemed? Wickham and Mr. Collins were evil and Mr. Darcy was good!

Wickham raised his arm that held the pistol. "Get away from her. I warn you I am much inclined to shoot you then have Elizabeth next."

Mr. Darcy flinched with how carelessly Wickham threw out that he planned to ravage Elizabeth, his own beloved wife. Wickham had forever been a thorn in his side. Mr. Darcy scowled at that smug, smirking reprobate and vowed he would die before Wickham touched a hair on Elizabeth's head. He had to get her away from there.

"Elizabeth, please get on my horse and go. You need to get away from here. My horse will know the way back to Netherfield." Mr. Darcy did not take his eyes off Wickham's pistol.

"I cannot leave you! I cannot run away and leave you to face men with pistols!" Elizabeth's fear was overcome by her anger at the thought of running away like a coward while Mr. Darcy sacrificed himself.

"No indeed, Elizabeth, I do not want you to leave. Mr. Collins was not supposed to start without me." Wickham smirked at Elizabeth.

Elizabeth's face reddened. "You are a despicable, worthless wastrel! You fool everyone into thinking you are a gentleman, but in fact you are the worst kind of scoundrel!"

Mr. Darcy had continued to back up a step at a time with Elizabeth, towards Mr. Collins. He only needed a moment's distraction. "What George Wickham has failed to tell you, amongst his many stories," said Mr. Darcy, "is that he is a notorious liar, a cheat and a scoundrel. I grew up with him at Pemberley as he was the son of my late father's steward. I also went to Cambridge with him where I had the misfortune to learn more of his dissolute behaviors."

"You were always the stick in the mud, Fitzwilliam. Never wanted to join in our fun." Wickham smiled and winked at Elizabeth.

Elizabeth's anger overcame her fear. How horrible was that Wickham! A headache bothered her now from her continued scowling.

"Ravaging chambermaids is not and has never been my idea of fun. Nor is kidnapping my sister to force an elopement." Mr. Darcy continued to step backwards.

Elizabeth gasped.

Wickham smiled. "Yes, the lovely Georgiana Darcy. It is too bad you care for her so much, Fitzwilliam, and showed up a day early to Ramsgate. We should have been married and the Darcy fortune in my hands before you ever found out. Well, I have a new plan to get that fortune now."

Elizabeth gasped at the depth of evil that Wickham had admitted to. She stepped back and nearly fell but caught herself on Mr. Darcy's coat. "Oh, I stepped on Mr. Collins."

"And what is your plan, Wickham? To kill me and Elizabeth to get your hands on the Darcy fortune? Georgiana will not be so easy to convince for an elopement." Mr. Darcy continued to wait for an opening, a chance to change this meeting to his favor. Now he knew they were in the right position, next to Mr. Collins, any moment he could grab the pistol Mr. Collins had dropped and turn things to his favor.

"Oh come now Fitzwilliam, do I need a plan? Or will simple revenge suffice?" Wickham smiled. "I will console Georgiana and she will marry me of her own accord or with a little help from a bottle. See, Fitzwilliam, you stopped nothing. I have it all under control."

Mr. Darcy tried to calm his rage as he did not want to make any stupid moves, not with a pistol centered on him and his wife to protect. He just needed one moment of distraction on Wickham's part to even the odds.

Elizabeth trembled with rage at the worthless scoundrel she had liked and hoped to marry at one time. She did not know much about horses, but Elizabeth knew they startled easily. She reached to the bonnet ribbons against her neck as her bonnet was lying against her back. She untied the ribbons, slowly dragged the bonnet into her hand and threw it at Wickham's horse with a scream.

The effects were instantaneous. Wickham's horse reared and jumped sideways which caused Wickham to focus on staying in the saddle. But, Mr. Darcy's horse also startled and ran out of the little meadow.

"Run, Elizabeth!" Mr. Darcy screamed as he bent down to find and grab Mr. Collins' pistol.

Wickham lost control and fell off his horse.

Elizabeth turned back to Mr. Darcy and saw him with a pistol in his hand rush past her to where Wickham was on the ground. Elizabeth did not want to leave Mr. Darcy, but she also did not want to be anywhere near Wickham or Mr. Collins. After prevaricating she finally obeyed her husband and ran out of the little meadow.

But then she stopped running. Elizabeth could not leave Mr. Darcy to face Wickham alone. What if something horrible happened? She would forever blame herself that she had left like a coward. Elizabeth knew Mr. Darcy could shoot a rifle, but could he shoot a pistol? Wickham was a soldier and trained to shoot a pistol. Mr. Darcy could be dead within minutes if they dueled.

Elizabeth ran back towards the little meadow. She slowed to a walk as she reached the meadow and crept amongst the trees. Neither man turned their head towards her even though she could not have been quiet running through the trees to the meadow.

Elizabeth heard Wickham taunt Mr. Darcy but did not hear her husband reply. She carefully crept through the trees around the men who were focused on each other. Elizabeth stopped when she was to the side and slightly behind Wickham.

"You have ruined things again, Fitzwilliam. You are ever interfering in my life. Why will you not leave me alone? I will have to get rid of you once and for all." Wickham stopped circling, stood still and raised his arms to a shooting stance.

This would not do! Wickham would not kill her husband, not when she could do something about it. Elizabeth darted out of the trees and screamed just as she heard the loud retort of a pistol. She pushed Wickham's side. He was easy to push over but then she tripped and fell on top of Wickham with the wind knocked out of her.

"Elizabeth!" Mr. Darcy's strangled cry tore at Elizabeth's heart. Mr. Darcy had been horrified when he saw Elizabeth run out of the trees to push Wickham. He had just shot his pistol at that cretin!

Elizabeth could not answer as she still could not breathe yet. She longed to get off of that foul Wickham but she had not yet recovered from her hard landing. She heard the pounding of footsteps, then was rolled over so she faced up at her husband.

Mr. Darcy glanced at Elizabeth's chest and howled.

CHAPTER 31

A large red stain was on Elizabeth's jacket and dress over her chest. She laid still on Wickham's legs.

"No! Elizabeth! Why did you run when I shot at Wickham? Elizabeth, I love you so much. You cannot die on me please, Elizabeth!" Mr. Darcy tore off his jacket and pushed it against Elizabeth's chest over the center of the red circle of blood.

He leaned down and cradled Elizabeth's upper body with his other arm. Tears ran down his cheeks to drip on her hair. He would never forgive himself if Elizabeth died due to his bullet. Not the woman he had admired for months and had just married.

"I worried that he would shoot you." Elizabeth's voice was faint.

"Do not waste your strength. I am sure help will be here soon. Wickham's horse should have gone back to his stable and mine back to Netherfield. Stay calm." Mr. Darcy glanced all over her face as if memorizing her features.

"But Fitzwilliam---" Elizabeth longed to tell him her important news, but his pressure on her chest was too great for her to speak.

"No, do not talk. Do not waste your energy." Mr. Darcy choked back a sob. "I am so sorry, Elizabeth. I did not know you would push him to save me. I would never have fired had I seen you. Oh, Elizabeth, I love you. I cannot lose you when I just found you!" Mr. Darcy choked on his tears and could not speak anymore. He rocked back and forth while he leaned over Elizabeth.

It was hard for her to breathe with the pressure Mr. Darcy exerted. She could only stare at Mr. Darcy's countenance as tears ran down his face and he told her how much he loved her. She tried to speak but Mr. Darcy did not hear her. If only he could hear her! "I am---"

A shadow fell over them and Mr. Darcy looked up. His agony turned to horror when he saw Mr. Collins with a pistol trained on him. Mr. Collins held his other hand over his left eye and raised welt on his cheek. "I do not want to do this, Mr. Darcy, but you made me. I am ever Lady Catherine de Bourgh's obedient servant even against you, her beloved nephew. She is most displeased with you as she stated in her letter to me but now that you have attacked me, and stolen my wife who is so far beneath you, you will be punished most severely."

Mr. Darcy did not like the look in Mr. Collins' eye. It was not the look of a sane man. They were unpredictable, unable to care or follow any rules only seeking their vengeance at the expense of everything else. He had to protect Elizabeth from this mad man. He had to distract him somehow. "Mr. Collins, get help for Elizabeth!"

"You took away what should have been mine!" Mr. Collins grew even more agitated. He lowered his arm so that the pistol was only an arm's length away from Mr. Darcy's head. Mr. Collins then turned his head towards the sound of hoofbeats, many hoofbeats that rapidly came nearer.

Mr. Darcy did not know how many others were involved in the plot that Mr. Collins and Wickham had planned. He hoped with all his might those horses were help and not more ruffians to subdue and kill him and Elizabeth. He would not let that happen.

"Do the right thing and help Elizabeth! You are a man of the cloth!" Mr. Darcy stared at Mr. Collins, whose arm holding the pistol wavered. "If you do not get help and she dies, then by God, I will strip the skin off of you, dunk you in a barrel of saltwater until you beg for mercy, and *I will not give it.*" Mr. Darcy's growl caused Mr. Collins to retreat several steps, though he did not lower his pistol.

"Lady Catherine de Bourgh will reward me! She said you have forever polluted Pemberley by marrying that hussy far beneath you! She is most displeased with you and will reward me for getting rid of this mess you created!" Mr. Collins stepped towards Mr. Darcy again, his arm up and a pistol pointed not at Mr. Darcy, but at Elizabeth.

The thundering of hooves was so loud that speech was impossible to be heard. Mr. Collins turned towards the direction of the sound to see militia men on horseback burst into the little clearing.

"Ho, you there! Drop your pistol!" Militia men jumped off their horses and subdued Mr. Collins.

Mr. Darcy nearly sagged in relief, but he could not rest as his beautiful wife's life hung in the balance. "I need my wife taken to a physician! She has been shot!"

Mr. Darcy refused offers to retrieve his carriage, instead insisting that Mrs. Darcy be transported immediately in the only available conveyance, a dirty militia wagon. He also refused to let anyone else hold Elizabeth, except for the brief time it took for him to climb into the back of the wagon. Then he reached his arms out for Elizabeth, and yelled at the driver to take them to the surgeon like the hounds of hell were after him.

He looked down at Elizabeth, at her pale countenance, the fear in her eyes and willed the horses to run faster, to fly over the countryside as fast as they could. Mr. Darcy braced himself as much as possible so that Elizabeth would feel little jostling. He pushed as hard as he could on her chest and hoped he had stopped the blood loss. He prayed as they raced to Meryton. "Please save my love! Please save my Elizabeth!"

The ___shire militia headquartered in Meryton had been the site of medical training that week. A surgeon had worked with medical staff to train some militia men on rudimentary medical skills. As luck would have it, the surgeon and entire medical staff were prepared for their arrival. They leapt into action before the wagon had stopped.

"Save her!" Mr. Darcy handed Elizabeth to a young man and jumped off the wagon. He had to be near Elizabeth, to hold her hand, to let her know she was not alone.

Mr. Darcy rushed into the medical building, but was stopped by a member of the militia. "This is no place for you, sir. Please wait outside."

Mr. Darcy realized he was not acting in a manner befitting one of his station. He stood and straightened his clothing. "I must be with my wife. She has to be terrified."

"We are sorry, sir. This man will lead you to the officer's room where you can wait."

Mr. Darcy scowled.

WITH THE PRESSURE of Mr. Darcy's hand removed from her chest, Elizabeth could finally take several deep breaths. She had to alert the medical men before they started to cut into her. "I was not shot. I am fine."

The men ignored her as they strapped her to the table. She thought for sure they would have stopped their preparations. Now, she was scared and getting more terrified as a man leaned over her with a foul-smelling cloth. "I tell you, this is not my blood! I am fine and perfectly well!"

The man held the cloth to her nose. She turned her head but it was held firm. They were going to cut into her even though it was not needed. She had to get them to listen or they would kill her!

CHAPTER 32

"STOP! I HAVE NOT BEEN SHOT!" Elizabeth's scream finally stopped their frantic preparations.

"You are mistaken. There is a large blood spot on your clothing. We must operate quickly." The surgeon looked away from Elizabeth and motioned to the man with the foul-smelling cloth to hold it over her nose again.

"Look at my jacket! Look at my dress! There is no hole, there was no bullet! I am perfectly fine. Please do not operate on me!" Elizabeth was terrified. If she could not get them to stop, she very well would die on this table. Oh, please let them listen to me, she prayed!

The surgeon leaned over and lifted her jacket. He unbuttoned it, then lifted her dress away from her body. The light of the room and the eyes of the staff saw the truth. "There is no bullet hole! Why did you not state this before? The entire regiment raced to save your life."

"Because my husband was pushing so hard on my chest to stop what he thought was a bullet wound, I could not speak. Please, let me up. I want to be with my husband, Mr. Darcy." Elizabeth would not breathe easy until she was far away from that room, the table with the straps and that foul-smelling cloth. But, the men stood around the table and stared at her. Would they not let her go?

"If that is not your blood, then whose is it?" The surgeon pointed to the large circle of drying blood on Elizabeth's jacket and dress.

"It is George Wickham's."

~

Mr. Darcy sat in the officer's room with his head down, cradled in his hands. He willed himself to stop the flow of tears, but it was futile. How could this happen to them? He had married the woman that had occupied his thoughts for the last several weeks and now she was on the verge of death. Or, was she dead already.

He wiped his eyes and swallowed the brandy a soldier had set beside him. If only she would survive, to live, to be with him forever. He would spend the rest of his life making it up to her.

The door to the room opened. Mr. Darcy looked up and blanched. It was a specter. The ghost of his late wife, Elizabeth, stood before him and then began to walk towards him in her torn and bloody clothes. "She is gone. I am seeing her ghost. Oh Elizabeth, I have failed you!"

The specter continued to walk towards Mr. Darcy with a smile and her hands outstretched. Mr. Darcy sat up with widened eyes. "I am perfectly well, Fitzwilliam. It was not I that you shot, but Wickham. When he fell, I tripped and could not catch my breath to tell you I was fine. Then with your pressure on my chest to save my life, I could not speak then either as the pressure was so strong."

Mr. Darcy reached up, touched her arms, her hair and her face. He stood and held her hands. "You are perfectly well? Truly, I did not shoot you?"

Elizabeth smiled and hugged Mr. Darcy. She squeezed him tighter and shivered as she fought her lingering terror over how close she had come to being cut open. "I am so glad we are both well. I was so scared and then I could not speak to tell anyone that I was not shot."

Mr. Darcy held her tight, laid his head upon hers and held her. Her scent, the feel of her arms around him. He would never forget this wonderful feeling that she was alive and his. "I thought I had lost you."

Elizabeth smiled against his chest. "I know. I heard everything you said." Elizabeth looked up. "I realize it was the heat of the moment and you thought I had died but---"

"I meant every word, Elizabeth." Mr. Darcy pulled back enough to look into her eyes. He was so lucky to have Elizabeth hale and hearty in his arms.

Tears gathered in Elizabeth's eyes as she gazed in wondrous happiness at the man who not only had saved her from a disastrous marriage, but from two malevolent men, as well. And he loved her too. She was so lucky to be in his arms and married to him.

A throat cleared. "Pardon me, but the Lord Lieutenant and magistrate are waiting to talk to you. If you will come this way." The soldier raised his arm towards the doorway.

"My wife has undergone a horrible ordeal and is still in her ruined clothes. I shall escort her to Netherfield. The Lord Lieutenant and the magistrate can interview her tomorrow." Mr. Darcy still held Elizabeth within his arms. "Send word to Netherfield for the carriage."

"Please Mr. Darcy, if you would come this way."

Elizabeth smiled up at her husband. She had been so wrong about him. Mr. Darcy was not the horrible man that Wickham had made him out to be. She had not had time to come to terms with what Wickham had revealed about his and Darcy's past but she had already known Mr. Darcy did not match what Wickham had said about him.

Mr. Darcy and Elizabeth were ushered into an office. Mr. Darcy did not let go of Elizabeth during the walk to the room or even after they sat in chairs in front of a desk. Mr. Darcy had to reassure himself that she was perfectly well and alive. Elizabeth held onto Mr. Darcy like a lifeline thrown to swimmers. He would keep her safe.

Elizabeth drank a cup of tea before she began to describe what had happened that day. Mr. Darcy continued the story, picking up after Elizabeth pushed Wickham so he could not shoot Mr. Darcy. The Lord Lieutenant had already heard from the officers that had come upon the scene. He was not surprised by Mr. Wickham's behavior.

Elizabeth shuddered at what it meant that the Lord Lieutenant had not been surprised at Wickham's actions. What else had he done? How had all the gentry of Meryton been so fooled and taken in by that man?

Mr. Collins was currently being held by the magistrate. The magistrate had been to Longbourn earlier that day to arrest Mr. Collins but did not find him. The magistrate searched for Mr. Collins when he heard the commotion made by the militia and reports of the scene they had found. Now Mr. Collins had more crimes added to his list of offenses. He would be in gaol for some time.

The magistrate planned to hold a Petty Session to hear the details of these crimes from all witnesses. The magistrate assured Mr. Darcy that from what he had just heard, Mr. Collins' crimes were severe enough to warrant being heard at the next Assizes Courts. Since they were held infrequently, two or three times a year, Mr. Collins had quite a wait for the next one.

"What will become of Longbourn?" Elizabeth leaned forward. "Will it revert to my family?"

The magistrate cleared his throat. "You will need to meet with an attorney regarding Longbourn's entailment. I would imagine the estate would go to the next male heir as the charges against Mr. Collins are such that he has been stripped of his property. Hanging or transportation are the only punishments available to him."

Elizabeth blanched. To hear of those punishments was one thing, but to have someone you knew suffer that fate, was quite unsettling. It was no less than he deserved though. Elizabeth worried at her new-found bloodthirsty thoughts, but Mr. Darcy distracted her by squeezing her hand.

"I am glad Mr. Collins is in custody. His fate will be one he fully deserves." Mr. Darcy stood and helped Elizabeth up from her chair.

Elizabeth wore Mr. Darcy's jacket over her soiled clothes as they walked to their waiting carriage. Mr. Darcy helped Elizabeth into the carriage and then joined her. Finally, they were on their way back home.

CHAPTER 33

Elizabeth stared at Mr. Darcy who sat next to her in the carriage. Elizabeth no longer worried that he regretted his hasty marriage or thought of getting an annulment. She would never forget his words that proclaimed how much he loved and could not live without her.

Mr. Darcy turned towards Elizabeth. At this close distance, Elizabeth could see his eyes were a beautiful shade of golden brown. "Are you in any pain?" he asked. "I can have the carriage slow down if the speed is causing you discomfort."

Elizabeth shook her head and smiled. Her smile was lopsided as her right cheek was swollen and bruised from where Mr. Collins had struck her. "The carriage is not causing me any pain."

Mr. Darcy's full lips curled up into a smile. "I know you enough by now, Elizabeth, to know that since you avoided my question, it means you are in pain."

Elizabeth's eyes twinkled. "How well you know me, sir. But the speed of the carriage is not causing any more pain to my injuries."

Mr. Darcy focused on Elizabeth's swollen right cheek. "I wish I could beat that man for eternity for what he did to you."

Elizabeth put her hand on Mr. Darcy's thigh. He stilled, scarcely allowed himself to breathe, so that his heightened emotions would cool. This was not the time or place to show his appreciation of his wife's touch.

Elizabeth looked at Mr. Darcy. "I believe he will be satisfactorily punished enough by being in the gaol, and being sentenced for his crimes. The embarrassment of losing his living, losing Longbourn, and losing the admiration of his patroness, along with the scorn of the people of Meryton, will affect him greatly. Plus, he will face transportation or hanging."

Elizabeth moved her hand back. "I do wish to know if Longbourn will belong to my family again."

Mr. Darcy adjusted his position on the bench. "Are there any other male heirs besides Mr. Collins? I would imagine Longbourn would go to the next male heir."

"I do not know of any. I hope Mr. Phillips can find one. I would not want Longbourn to go to the Crown and sold at an auction."

"If it came to that, I believe Mr. Bingley and I would step in to save your family home." Mr. Darcy squeezed Elizabeth's hand.

"Thank you, Fitzwilliam." There were so many surprises from that day, but the one that was uppermost in Elizabeth's mind was how much she admired Mr. Darcy. She even felt she was well on her way to falling in love with him.

ELIZABETH AND MR. DARCY walked into an uproar at Netherfield.

"You must find him! Oh, my poor nerves! To have lost a wealthy son-in-law so soon!" Mrs. Bennet wailed so loud she could be heard in the foyer.

"Get out there and find him! Use whatever is at your disposal. Horses, carriages, men. Just find him!" Miss Bingley's voice no longer was the dulcet voice she used when she wanted to impress. No, this was more like a fishmonger's wife.

Elizabeth and Mr. Darcy looked at each other with widened eyes. No one must have heard the footman exclaim they were back.

Mr. Darcy turned to the footman. "Where is Mr. Bingley?"

"He is leading the search for you, sir."

Mr. Darcy narrowed his eyes. "Search? Why is there a search for me?"

"Your horse came back without you, sir."

Mr. Darcy grinned and looked at Elizabeth.

"He is a well-trained horse, Mr. Darcy." Elizabeth patted his chest as Mr. Darcy's grin widened. He pulled Elizabeth into an embrace. After thinking he had lost her earlier, he felt the need to reassure himself that she was well. He could not imagine life without her.

Mr. Darcy raised his head. "Have a hot bath drawn for Mrs. Darcy. She will also need a poultice for swelling. And fetch the housekeeper, Mrs. Ponds, for me."

The footman bowed and hurried off.

Mr. Darcy and Elizabeth pulled apart. She put her hand on his arm and they walked into the drawing room.

Mrs. Hurst noticed them first. "Oh, Mr. Darcy? You are well!"

Mrs. Bennet sat up and screamed. "Mr. Darcy! You are alive and well! Oh, I knew you would be safe! Did I not say that? I told--"

Miss Bingley turned around, rushed to Mr. Darcy and did not even spare a glance for Elizabeth. "Oh, Mr. Darcy thank goodness you are well! We were so worried when your horse came to Netherfield without you. Are you injured? I shall--"

Mr. Darcy scowled. "Miss Bingley, as you can see, I am perfectly fine. However, my wife is wearing torn and bloodied clothing."

Elizabeth fought her smile while Miss Bingley flushed and glanced at her.

Jane squeezed Elizabeth's hand. "Elizabeth, what happened to you? Are you injured?"

Elizabeth shook her head and hugged Jane. "I am well. There was a mishap during my walk." She glanced at Mr. Darcy and then leaned in to Jane. "I will tell you more later."

Kitty and Lydia surrounded Elizabeth and clamored to know what happened. "I will tell you later."

"If you will excuse us, Elizabeth needs to change and rest now." Mr. Darcy bowed to the room then led his wife to the stairs where they encountered the housekeeper.

"I heard Mr. Bingley and staff left to search for me. Can you send a man to let them know I am well? Have Mr. Bingley come to me when he gets back." Mr. Darcy turned and helped Elizabeth up the stairs which turned out to be difficult due to her bruises from fighting off Mr. Collins.

ELIZABETH FELT MUCH BETTER after her hot bath. The poultice eased the swelling on her cheek as well. She sneaked glances at her husband as she laid on the bed. "Fitzwilliam, I am curious on a few points related to today's events." Elizabeth swallowed and curled her hands in the bedsheets. "Today, you said you love me, and I believe have loved me for some time. Why did you not court me, or offer for me earlier? And do not tell me again that Mr. Collins was not worthy of me."

Mr. Darcy walked to her bedside. "I have no excuse, Elizabeth."

Elizabeth waited but though Mr. Darcy was agitated, he did not speak. Elizabeth regretted her choice of topic, especially after they had both suffered during the earlier ordeal. "I apologize, Fitzwilliam. I am overwhelmed by the day, I do not know what prompted me to bring that up. Please forgive me. I shall sleep now."

Mr. Darcy let out a long sigh and shook his head. "No, Elizabeth. I owe you the truth." He took a breath. "I... I fear that if I tell you, you will no longer be pleased with me. That you may look upon me with disgust." He raised his head and stared at Elizabeth.

Elizabeth furrowed her brow. "I cannot imagine anything that would cause me to do so."

Mr. Darcy twitched his lips and cleared this throat. "I have admired you for some time, but your family's... behavior and social standing prevented me from acknowledging my feelings."

"My father was a gentleman and I am a gentleman's daughter. We are in the same social standing."

Mr. Darcy's face was pinched. "I do not want to cause you any pain, Elizabeth. But your younger sisters, your mother have behaved with a lack of decorum and propriety. The inferiority of your connections and my role as caretaker of Pemberley and the Darcy name prevented me from pursuing you."

Elizabeth's color had heightened during Mr. Darcy's explanation. "I see. It is a wonder that you married me at all!"

Mr. Darcy sat down next to Elizabeth. She attempted to roll away but Mr. Darcy's hand on her shoulder prevented it. "Elizabeth, I did not want to cause you any distress, but I also do not want to be less than honest with you. You heard what I said today, yelled in fact, in front of the entire militia. That I love you, and I cannot live without you."

Elizabeth stayed quiet. Her exhaustion, shock at the events of the day had caused her usual sensibleness to be overcome. It hurt to hear criticism of her family even though she knew what Mr. Darcy said was true.

"I believe you have gone through a horrible ordeal today and are not yourself. I will leave you to sleep." Mr. Darcy stood.

Elizabeth turned her head and watched Mr. Darcy walk to the door. He put his hand on the doorknob but looked back at Elizabeth. He stood and stared at her as she stared at him. A tear rolled down the bruised cheek.

Mr. Darcy let go of the doorknob and walked back to Elizabeth. "I cannot stand to see you in such distress. Let me join you."

Mr. Darcy pulled at his coat sleeves, then put his arms behind his back and pulled at the sleeves. He tugged and moved his arms closer together, even contorted his body to tug harder to remove his jacket. He stopped when he heard giggles.

"I apologize, but the faces you were making, the contortions---" Elizabeth laughed.

Mr. Darcy's lips twitched, then he smiled as he admitted that he did look rather ridiculous. He let go of the jacket sleeves, which had barely moved. "That coat is so snug I cannot get it off without help."

Mr. Darcy walked to the bell pull.

"Wait! You do not need to call your valet as I will help you." Elizabeth got out of bed.

"I do not want you to exert yourself, Elizabeth. You are injured." Mr. Darcy turned as Elizabeth reached him.

"I am well enough to act as your valet." Elizabeth tugged at the coat and pulled it off one of Mr. Darcy's arms. She tugged the other sleeve, and the coat was off.

"I thank you. I would prefer you as my valet." Mr. Darcy smiled.

"I fear I cannot take care of your clothes, or dress you as well as your valet can. His job is safe." Elizabeth smiled at Mr. Darcy and blushed. "I must apologize for questioning you earlier. It was certainly not the time for it."

Mr. Darcy wrapped his arms around Elizabeth. "You have nothing to apologize for. It was a horrible ordeal you suffered today. Let me change and I will join you in bed."

Elizabeth looked up at Mr. Darcy. "Thank you. I have a request though. Would you hold me?"

Mr. Darcy cleared his throat and nodded. He changed into his nightshirt and joined Elizabeth in bed. "If you would roll onto your side, I could hold you."

Elizabeth rolled onto her side with her back to Mr. Darcy. He tentatively draped an arm over her waist. They laid like that for a few minutes, then Elizabeth scooted backwards. Mr. Darcy moved back as well. Elizabeth scooted back again which prompted Mr. Darcy to move back as well.

Elizabeth rolled onto her back and looked at him. "Why are you moving away from me?"

Mr. Darcy cleared his throat. "I would think you would want a space between us."

Elizabeth frowned. "I want to be held by you."

Mr. Darcy adjusted the opening of his nightshirt. "I do not think you would want me to lie too close to you." Elizabeth scowled. "There are some... things you do not know yet as we have not had our wedding night."

Elizabeth's eyebrows rose. "Such as what? I am curious to know why you cannot hold your wife."

Mr. Darcy sighed. "If I held you, I could not prevent my body from reacting to you."

Elizabeth's eyebrows rose higher. "In what way?"

Mr. Darcy flattened his lips and wished that Elizabeth was not so curious. Though he would not have her any other way. "It would be difficult for me to not want to... proceed to the wedding night."

"Oh." Elizabeth stared at Mr. Darcy as a blush rose in her cheeks. "Mr. Collins tried to ravage me and Wickham said that they had planned---"

"Do not speak of it, Elizabeth. It pains you." Mr. Darcy frowned as it pained him that those scoundrels had attempted to ravage his Elizabeth.

"I do not want it to pain me! I want to overcome it. I want new memories to replace those. Memories of you, my husband. I want to have our wedding night."

Mr. Darcy stilled. "I do not think that would be a good idea. You are sore and injured from today. Let us wait--"

Elizabeth rolled onto her side and faced Mr. Darcy. "No. No more waiting. We have learned about each other since our wedding. Today I learned more about you, your character and your feelings for me than the past days combined." Elizabeth reached out and placed her hand on Mr. Darcy's arm.

"Elizabeth, I do not want to hurt you."

"Then do not say no."

They stared at each other. Then, Mr. Darcy blinked and let out his breath. "I cannot turn down the most beautiful woman in the world. I do not have that much strength."

Mr. Darcy opened his eyes to Elizabeth's smile.

CHAPTER 34

Elizabeth and Mr. Darcy enjoyed a lie-in the next morning. They continued to share confidences and learn about each other well into the day. It was not until later, after they ate dinner in their room, that they walked downstairs to the sitting room where the majority of the house's inhabitants were situated.

"Oh, finally you are up!" said Lydia. "You will not believe what we heard, that Mr. Collins is in the gaol and will lose Longbourn!"

Kitty sat up on the sofa. "And that George Wickham has been shot! But no one--"

Lydia turned and leaned over Kitty. "I was telling the news! Keep your breath to cool your porridge." Lydia turned back to Elizabeth and Mr. Darcy. "The most scandalous news is that George Wickham was shot, but no one knows anything else. I bet he was shot climbing out of Miss King's room."

Elizabeth gaped at her youngest sister. This behavior would not be appropriate in their own house of Longbourn, but in the house of a brother-in-law it was preposterous. "Lydia! Control yourself and remember where you are."

"Mr. Bingley is our brother now and I can act how I want amongst family." Lydia stuck her chin out.

Elizabeth gasped. Footsteps sounded close behind so Elizabeth turned to see who had overheard Lydia's horrible display. She flushed as Jane and Mr. Bingley stepped into the room.

Mr. Bingley scowled at Lydia. "Lydia, you are my sister-in-law now but you are a guest in my home. I will not allow you to behave in this manner. You will behave with the proper decorum or you will be sent to your room!"

Silence reigned. Lydia blanched and gaped at Mr. Bingley. Kitty scooted away from her on the sofa.

Miss Bingley looked with disgust at the Bennet sisters. She then turned to her brother and approached their group with a smile. "Charles, how glad am I to see you."

Mr. Bingley nodded to his sister. "Thank you, Caroline." He turned to Mr. Darcy and Elizabeth. "I am most interested in hearing that you are well with no injuries?"

"We are well, thank you." Mr. Darcy answered.

"Please, come and sit with us. I have heard rumors but nothing that I believe resembles the truth. Tell us what led to your horse coming back to Netherfield without you? Nothing short of some severe calamity could cause Mr. Darcy to become unseated." Mr. Bingley led the way to a grouping of chairs.

The other inhabitants of the room stood up and moved closer. Mrs. Bennet asked a footman to move a chair so she could be included in the grouping.

Jane hugged Elizabeth. "Are you well? I have been so worried about you."

"Thank you." Elizabeth sat next to Mr. Darcy. "I am well and much recovered." A blush crawled up Elizabeth's visage and she glanced at Mr. Darcy with a sparkle in her eye.

"Tell us, Lizzy, do not keep us in suspense any longer," said Mrs. Bennet. "Mr. Darcy's horse gave us quite a fright and then our carriage was called for by a member of the militia!"

Mr. Darcy took Elizabeth's hand. "You need not share if it discomforts you."

Elizabeth squeezed his hand and smiled. "I do not want that event to rule my behavior." She faced her family. "Mr. Collins assaulted me while I rambled along my usual walking path." Gasps filled the air. "But Fitzwilliam came to my rescue. Mr. Wickham..." She pursed her lips. "We have all been taken in by Mr. Wickham. He had planned it all with Mr. Collins. They were to... ravage me... then kill me in revenge on Mr. Darcy."

"Wickham?" Mrs. Bennet brought a hand to her chest. "Why I knew there was something off about that man! Remember when I said--"

"Wickham?" Lydia exclaimed. "He would not do such a thing! Why are you---"

Mr. Darcy stood. "My wife is not in the habit of telling falsehoods." He scowled at Lydia.

Mr. Bingley also stood with a reddened countenance. "Lydia, you are banished to your room for the remainder of this day! I expect you to comport yourself as befits the daughter of a gentleman. If you cannot do so you will not be allowed at Netherfield."

Lydia gaped, turned to Mrs. Bennet who looked away and then burst into tears as she ran out of the room.

Elizabeth released a breath, smiled at Mr. Darcy and squeezed his hand. "Thank you."

"Thank you, Charles." Jane held Mr. Bingley's hand.

"I am glad that did not offend you, Jane, but by Jove she ---!" Mr. Bingley cleared his countenance when he saw Mrs. Bennet. He cleared his throat. "Well."

Jane spoke. "And so is it true? Mr. Collins is in gaol?" Jane asked.

Elizabeth nodded. "Yes. We met with the Lord Lieutenant and magistrate. Mr. Collins will be held until the next Assizes Court."

"And Wickham? The militia's punishment will certainly be worse." Mr. Bingley looked at Mr. Darcy.

Mr. Darcy squeezed Elizabeth's hand. "Mr. Wickham held a pistol on us. I shot and killed him." Gasps filled the air.

"Oh! Oh, my Lizzy!" Mrs. Bennet exclaimed. "Oh my nerves! To have a pistol trained upon you and by none other than that odious Mr. Collins!" Mrs. Bennet fell back in her chair. "My nerves, such flutterings. Bring the smelling salts!"

Elizabeth and Mr. Darcy shared a look and then accepted the hugs and well wishes from the room's inhabitants that they had survived a pair of obviously deranged men.

Mr. Bingley shook his friend's hand. "You were not even hurt? Only you could take down two men without a scratch!"

"I fear Elizabeth suffered the brunt. I would gladly have taken her place." Mr. Darcy frowned.

"I am glad you both escaped those madmen. I cannot imagine... What is to become of Longbourn, then? Surely Mr. Collins will be hanged or transported?"

Mr. Darcy shook his head. "Mr. Collins will have been stripped of all his belongings by now. Longbourn should go to the next male heir of Mr. Bennet. If one is not found, then it would revert to the Crown and sold at auction."

Mrs. Bennet turned towards the men. "Mr. Collins has lost Longbourn! Do you hear that girls? We will have Longbourn again!" She hugged her girls. "Two of my girls married wealthy men and we shall have Longbourn! I must write to my sister. Such a turn of events!"

"Mama! We may not have Longbourn," said Jane. "The next male heir of Papa needs to be found."

"Well, no relative of that horrible Mr. Collins should inherit what he stole from us," said Mrs. Bennet. "He destroyed all our belongings too! His relatives should not inherit at all! What good is punishment if his relatives end up profiting from his crime?"

Elizabeth shared a stare with Jane, then turned to Mrs. Bennet. "Mama, do you not want to move into the rental house in Meryton? Longbourn may not belong to our family. It could be months before we find out."

"Oh, why would I want to move into a small rental house when I can be back in Longbourn? It makes little sense to rent a house for such a short time."

Mr. Bingley cleared his throat. "Mrs. Bennet, do not worry about the financials. I shall have my steward lease the house you find most favorable. You could be in your new home as soon as the day after."

~

THE NEXT DAY showed to be another beautiful winter day with frost sparkling on everything.

"Elizabeth, would you care to walk with me on the grounds of Netherfield?" Mr. Darcy approached where she sat near the fireplace.

Elizabeth put down her book and turned to Mr. Darcy. She swallowed. She was hesitant to go outside and walk again. "Yes."

The Darcys walked companionably through the gardens. Though the plants and trees were bare of leaves and flowers, the landscape was a sparkling white monument to the artistry of winter.

"Thank you, Fitzwilliam, for getting me back outside." Elizabeth squeezed Mr. Darcy's arm.

"I care for you, Elizabeth, as you know." Mr. Darcy turned to her with a twinkle in his eye. "Plus I have heard that when you fall off a horse, it is best to get right back on."

Elizabeth tried not to smile but failed. "You are bound and determined to get me on the back of a horse, are you not, sir?"

"I love to ride, and I would dearly love to ride through the countryside with my wife by my side."

"You know I have little experience. As a matter fact I have none." Elizabeth smiled at her husband.

Mr. Darcy shook his head. "That does not matter, Elizabeth. I can find a pony or a horse perfect for a beginning rider."

"Are you insinuating that you will find an old horse perfect for young children or the infirm?"

Mr. Darcy turned to Elizabeth with widened eyes until he saw the twinkle in her eyes and a smirk on her lips. "That is exactly what I suggest, madam. A nice placid old horse that walks wherever it wants to go no matter how much you pull on the reins."

Elizabeth laughed. "Oh, Fitzwilliam! You would ride behind me laughing the entire time, would you not?"

"Not the entire time. At some point, I would lead the horse back to the stable." Mr. Darcy's lips twitched as he looked at Elizabeth.

Elizabeth laughed.

Mr. Darcy's countenance turned serious. "There is a question I would like to ask, and I am afraid it will cause you discomfort. What happened while you were at Longbourn?"

Elizabeth looked away. In the silence their boots were loud walking on the solid snow. "I have prevaricated enough times and you deserve an answer. When we found Mr. Collins would not marry who we had chosen and instead would only marry me, I declined his offer. I was confined to my room for several days until I relented and agreed to marry him."

Mr. Darcy's other hand covered hers and squeezed. Elizabeth glanced up at his scowling visage. "Whose idea was it to confine you to your room?"

"It does not matter now. It is over, and we are together thanks to your heroic deed of saving the maiden in distress."

Mr. Darcy looked at Elizabeth who smiled a fake grin. "I am glad that it is over and we are together, however, it affects you still. It was your mother who did that to you, was it not? No family should treat its members as such."

Elizabeth dropped her smile and looked away. It hurt her to remember that her own mother had treated her in that manner. And, that her younger sisters had berated her for days. "Understand that we were to be thrown out of our home just weeks after Papa died. My father did not save enough for us, so if we did not have Longbourn, we could only rent a small house if Jane and I were employed."

Mr. Darcy turned to Elizabeth. "I did not know it was bad as that, but that is still not an excuse for your treatment. Mr. Bennet did not save or prepare for his death though he knew Longbourn was entailed away from the family?"

"We did not find that out until after Papa's funeral when my uncle, Mr. Gardiner checked the finances. There was nothing to be done then. Jane and I, indeed our entire family, have you and Mr. Bingley to thank for our rescue." Elizabeth squeezed Mr. Darcy's arm. "Let us drop this. No good will come of dwelling upon what is in the past."

Mr. Darcy would not bring this up to Elizabeth again, but he had not made a promise not to share the information with his friend Mr. Bingley.

CHAPTER 35

Several letters were delivered to Netherfield. Mrs. Bennet read hers to the sitting room's inhabitants.

"My sister, Mrs. Phillips, writes that it is so sad that we are not at Longbourn any longer, as she cannot easily walk to see me. I would much rather she did that, instead of write to me, as she is not a good correspondent."

"Mama, what did she say about the officers?" Kitty put down her embroidery and leaned forward.

"Yes, is there any mention of Denny? I hope that Miss King has not latched onto him." Lydia turned to

Kitty with that bit of information. She spoke softly enough that it was not carried throughout the room. Mr. Bingley's punishment had managed to make an impression on Lydia.

Mrs. Bennet continued. "Oh, this is not good news. She says Mr. Phillips thinks it could take six months to a year to determine Mr. Bennet's closest male heir! That is too long." Mrs. Bennet looked up. "I wanted to be in Longbourn by May Day. Well, if it will take that long, I might as well take a different estate in Hertfordshire. If only I could get Croydon House. Everything is situated so well there."

Miss Bingley and Mrs. Hurst shared a long look.

Mrs. Bennet continued reading the letter. "Oh my, this is interesting. My sister writes that the magistrate has written the Bishop for inquiries into Mr. Collins' living relatives. What a horrible man. I knew the second I saw him he was evil. I had always told Mr. Bennet I did not want him to come to Longbourn at all, and was I not proven right?"

Elizabeth put down her book and stood. "I have sat for too long. I fear my legs are in need of a good stretch."

Jane put down her embroidery as well. "I feel the same. I believe we could have a good walk just by traversing the halls of Netherfield."

Mr. Darcy stood from shooting the billiard ball which bounced off one edge, knocked a ball into a hole, banked off another edge, and gently tapped another ball into a different hole.

"Zounds! How did you do that?" Mr. Bingley frowned at the billiard table.

Mr. Darcy turned to his friend. "It is just a matter of angles, Charles." Mr. Darcy smirked as he retrieved his glass of brandy.

"I daresay I could play for one hundred hours and still not be anywhere as good as you."

"Well, you are free to practice as much as you want, and I shall give you any help I can." Mr. Darcy drank his brandy and set it down as a footman entered the game room with a letter on a tray.

"There is a letter for you, sir."

Mr. Darcy took the envelope and saw it was from his aunt, Lady Catherine de Bourgh. He frowned. Had she learnt of his marriage?

While Mr. Bingley walked around the billiard table and muttered to himself about angles, Mr. Darcy sat down and read the letter.

Dear Nephew,

I have heard a report of the most alarming nature. That you have married without your relatives in attendance or even having knowledge of the event. But that is not the worst I heard. You stole the bride of another man on his wedding day! I would not think my nephew capable of such boorish behavior if the report had not come from the man whose bride you stole.

I am mortified that a close relative of mine could behave in such a scandalous manner. You have brought scandal to your relations! In doing so you ignored your fiancée, my daughter Anne, to whom you have been engaged since you were infants. You have embarrassed and shamed me with your behavior.

I send no greetings to your wife and do not extend an invitation for her to visit me at Rosings. I give no acknowledgment of that woman and offer no felicitations on this event.

Sincerely,

Lady Catherine de Bourgh

Mr. Darcy folded the letter. He wished he had done more to Mr. Collins when he had the chance. The petty vengeance of that man knew no bounds.

His aunt loved to get information first, therefore he would inform her of the whereabouts and actions of her choice for the living of Hunsford parsonage. Mr. Darcy begged the use of Mr. Bingley's study so he could write the letter.

Dear Lady Catherine,

Your information is correct, in that I married Elizabeth Bennet in Hertfordshire nearly a fortnight ago. I am the happiest of men as my wife is a beautiful, engaging and intelligent woman.

You will need to find another parson for the living at Hunsford parsonage as Mr. Collins is currently incarcerated in gaol awaiting his trial at the next Assizes. He is charged with the assault of my wife, theft, destruction of property, and attempted murder of myself and my wife. Because of the severity of his crimes, he will either be transported or hanged at Newgate. I hope you choose the next parson more wisely.

You are not welcome at any of my properties until you give my wife and I the respect we deserve.

Sincerely,

Fitzwilliam Darcy

Mr. Darcy folded the letter, sealed it with wax and pushed his signet ring in the cooling wax.

"You are done with your correspondence?" Mr. Bingley looked up from his chair, where he had been reading to pass the time while their wives walked.

"I am. I should not hear from my aunt for quite some time now."

Mr. Bingley held up his glass of brandy. "Here is to getting rid of quarrelsome relatives."

Mr. Darcy leaned back in the chair. "What are you going to do about the quarrelsome relatives currently living at Netherfield?"

Mr. Bingley sighed and rubbed his eyes. "I do not want to upset my beautiful bride, but I daresay I cannot stand one more day of Mrs. Bennet and those younger sisters."

Mr. Darcy twirled a quill in his hands. "I have news that may help you make your decision."

Mr. Bingley raised his eyebrows. "Do tell."

"Elizabeth told me she was confined to her room by Mrs. Bennet, after she refused to marry Mr. Collins. Mr. Collins had declared that he would marry her and no one else."

Mr. Bingley sat up in his chair. "Damnation! She was to marry him or he would throw them out of Longbourn?"

Mr. Darcy nodded. "Yes. I imagine the time was not pleasant for her, considering the outspoken natures of her younger sisters."

Mr. Bingley sat back in his chair with widened eyes. "By Jove, that is outrageous! And they are behaving abominably here too! I have a mind to turn them out on the morrow. Jane has already mentioned how upset she is by their behavior. Well, I will not have it anymore. Today is their last day at Netherfield."

CHAPTER 36

Elizabeth and Jane enjoyed themselves as they walked through Netherfield. "I did not know there were so many interesting portraits here. I regret we do not have a man as interesting as," Elizabeth leaned forward to peer at the brass plate on the frame, "Verne Nodcock." She stood up and raised her eyebrows at Jane. "We must find someone to remedy this oversight in our relations. Perhaps we could ask Mary or Kitty to marry only men with interesting names."

Jane laughed. "Oh Lizzy, I am so glad you are here with us at Netherfield. I do not know how I would fare without you."

"It has been a trial, has it not? Has Charles' steward found a house for Mama and our youngest sisters yet? I do not know if I can handle another minute in their company."

Jane sighed. "I think Lydia has gotten worse since Papa died. Mama is doing nothing about her behavior. Can she not see the looks the Bingley sisters give each other?"

Elizabeth frowned. "I am not so sure she sees their behavior as a problem."

Jane shook her head. "Charles is getting quite upset."

Elizabeth looked at Jane. "Perhaps they will be moving to their rental house soon?"

"Oh, I certainly hope so. I have enough to deal with from the Bingley sisters. I do not need my own younger sisters giving me fits."

"It must be bad, as I think I heard you say something critical?"

Jane looked askew at her sister. "I know you tease that I see the goodness in everyone all the time. But Elizabeth, I can no longer find any goodness in them. They are polite with perfect manners in company but when alone... their manners are horrible." Jane looked at Elizabeth. "The things they say about our neighbors and friends, you would not believe it. I have asked them to curb their unchristian behavior, but they only stopped when they thought I was within hearing."

"Jane, I am sorry you are being mistreated in your own home. Why do Mr. and Mrs. Hurst stay with their brother? Do they not have a house of their own?

"They do, a small townhouse in town, but they much prefer the amenities that come with Charles' inheritance."

"Well, of course, who would not prefer the better living that comes with more money?" Elizabeth and Jane looked at each other and giggled.

"Oh Elizabeth, you make everything better. If only Charles will too."

Elizabeth patted Jane's arm. "I am sure if he has the proper inducement, such as knowing how much his beloved wife is hurting, he will do the right thing.

Jane sighed. "I will talk to him again today. Maybe if I tell him his sisters and my family have affected me such that I am unwell."

Elizabeth giggled. "Oh Jane! I dare say that will do the trick posthaste."

Jane turned with a smile. "I hate to do that, but I know no other way."

Elizabeth hugged Jane's arm. "One does what one must."

THE NEXT DAY after everyone had broken their fast and were gathered in the sitting room, except for the Bingley sisters, Mr. Bingley and Jane entered the sitting room. "Mrs. Bennet," said Mr. Bingley, "I have leased a house for you in Meryton. You will again be mistress of your own house and Lydia and Kitty will have room to entertain themselves. The carriage will be available to move you to your new home in half an hour. My staff will have your house and foodstuffs ready for you by then." Mr. Bingley smiled.

Mrs. Bennet recovered. "Mr. Bingley, I expected that we would stay at Netherfield until we could move into Longbourn. Really, it is a waste for us to move into a rental house when we will only move to Longbourn soon after."

Elizabeth spoke. "Mama, we do not know if we will get Longbourn again. And we do not know how long it will take for them to research the next male heir."

Lydia jumped up from the sofa she shared with Kitty. "I love the idea! I cannot wait to be back in Meryton where all the exciting things happen. Come on, Kitty, let us pack." Both sisters walked out of the room and giggled as they ran upstairs.

Mrs. Bennet pursed her lips, then followed her daughters without a glance at the Bingleys.

Elizabeth frowned. The sooner her family, except Mary, was gone, the better. At least the Bingley sisters were not in the room to share looks and whisper to each other. If only they could be gotten rid of as easily.

"I think that went well." Mr. Bingley looked from Jane to Mr. Darcy.

Mr. Darcy nodded. "Well done, Charles."

Mr. Bingley smiled and then beamed as Jane leaned in and kissed his cheek.

Mary practiced on the pianoforte with the new sheet music Mr. Darcy had purchased for her. Even though Mary was not the best performer, Elizabeth was touched at Mr. Darcy's kindness. She squeezed his hand, and they both shared a look full of promise.

~

All the inhabitants of Netherfield turned out to see the Bennets off to their new home in Meryton. Lydia was no longer upset she could not stay at Netherfield. Indeed, she was happy to be away from her older sisters who corrected her behavior. Kitty was happy to be wherever Lydia was. Mary was relieved to be away from her younger sisters who embarrassed her.

Elizabeth turned to walk inside Netherfield and saw the Bingley sisters murmuring amongst themselves. She glanced at Jane, who rolled her eyes. Elizabeth smiled, and the sisters walked back into the house arm in arm.

She could not imagine being any happier than she was. The only thing that would have made her happier was for her father to not have died, except then Elizabeth would not have ever known how much Mr. Darcy loved her. Though she was sad her father's death was the catalyst, she was quite happy with the outcome.

Time would tell how often their mother left Meryton to visit them at Netherfield. Hopefully it would not be often. If it was, the Bingleys would just have to move. Elizabeth giggled.

Mr. Darcy leaned over. "Care to share what amused you?"

Elizabeth let go of Jane's arm and held onto her husband's. "I was wondering how often my mother might come to visit Netherfield. I thought if she visits too often, the Bingleys could move."

Mr. Darcy and Elizabeth looked at each other, then burst into laughter.

"And what of our leaving Netherfield? When will I see this famed estate with the grand library?" Elizabeth eyes twinkled as she looked at her husband.

"I had thought of staying here until the New Year. Then, I could bring my bride to her new home at the start of the new year. My sister, Georgiana, is with the Earl and Lady Matlock at their estate for the Christmas season. Pemberley will be ours for a month or two until she returns. It sounds silly, I apologize---"

Elizabeth squeezed Mr. Darcy's arm. "I love that idea. We will spend a few more weeks here with our friends and then leave for our home."

"I cannot wait to show you Pemberley."

They walked towards the sitting room but stopped at the sound of raised voices.

CHAPTER 37

"This is the last time I will tell you Caroline." said Mr. Bingley, "The Bennets are related to us by marriage now and you will treat them with respect. I do not want to hear you disparaging them again."

Miss Bingley's countenance changed to pinched lips. "This is my home too or have you forgotten that? You received the greatest share of our father's inheritance, as such you must provide for your sisters. I am not--"

"I cannot do that." Mr. Bingley said. "You have continued to disparage the Bennet family, even in front of them! I do not want to do this, but you will have to leave tomorrow. You can live with Louisa and Mr. Hurst in town, as they will also be leaving."

Mrs. Hurst gaped, then stood. "What have I done? Caroline is the one that mocked and criticized the Bennet family."

Mr. Bingley turned to his sister. "You joined in with Caroline and never tried to stop her. You know what-."

"That is no reason we cannot stay here at Netherfield." said Mrs. Hurst. "You have a house much bigger than the townhouse we have."

"That is enough." Mr. Bingley looked at both sisters. "Even if you stayed, you would not stop ridiculing the Bennets. You will both leave for town tomorrow."

Mrs. Hurst glared at her brother then stomped out of the sitting room turning her head away from the Darcys.

Miss Bingley glared at her brother. "You are required to provide for your sisters out of your inheritance. I am sure I can have a copy of the will sent from our family's attorney. You can not throw us out." Miss Bingley raised her head and smirked at Mr. Bingley.

Mr. Bingley stood taller. "Yes, I can! You should have thought of that before you continued to denigrate the Bennets. You have even been rude in front of them! I saw you laughing at Mrs. Bennet when she said I would buy an estate for her. You have not once tried to behave or ingratiate yourself with them. Since you cannot change your behavior, you will no longer live with me."

Miss Bingley scowled with flared nostrils and stormed out of the sitting room.

Mr. Darcy raised his eyebrows and walked with Elizabeth towards Mr. Bingley. "Well done, Charles."

Mr. Bingley threw himself in the nearest chair. "I can not understand why they do not realize the rudeness of their behavior?" Mr. Bingley looked up at Mr. Darcy with a smile. "Thank you, Darcy."

Elizabeth walked over to Jane who beamed. Elizabeth hugged her and then pulled back. "Your husband is quite a fierce knight."

"I know." Jane looked at Elizabeth and giggled. "Was he not wonderful?"

"He is the greatest of all men for taming the Bingley sisters." Elizabeth and Jane laughed.

Mr. Darcy sat across from his friend. "You should have peace here now."

Mr. Bingley twisted his lips. "I feel bad I yelled at my sisters. Was I too harsh?"

Jane walked over to Mr. Bingley. "I think you were wonderful, Charles."

Mr. Bingley held Jane's hand.

Elizabeth looked at the happy couple. "You will now be able to invite whatever friends and relatives you would like to dinner."

"Oh yes, that will be wonderful!" Jane said. "Now I can invite the Phillips and Lucas'."

Mr. Bingley looked at Jane. "You felt you could not?"

Jane flushed. "I... I did not want Caroline to behave as she had around them."

Mr. Bingley frowned and stood. "Jane, we must always talk and share everything. I do not want you to hide your concerns from me."

Jane's eyes widened, but she flushed when she caught Mr. Bingley's wink. The couple quit the sitting room.

Elizabeth turned to Mr. Darcy who had been watching her. "Shall we play a game? Sit next to each other and read our favorite books? Should I watch you write and comment on the beauty of your penmanship?"

Mr. Darcy's gaze grew heavy. "I would like to watch you play the pianoforte and sing."

Elizabeth smiled and chuckled. "You know I do not have the greatest skill at the pianoforte, or with singing. But if you want me to perform, I shall." Elizabeth leaned in and touched the tip of Mr. Darcy's nose. "You may need to cover your ears."

Mr. Darcy followed his wife to the corner where the pianoforte was situated. "I doubt that."

Miss. Bingley stormed to her bedchamber and slammed the door. "How dare Charles send me away from here! I know more about running a house fit for society than that country girl my brother married. She will make him a laughingstock!"

Miss Bingley picked her hairbrush up and threw it. "Blast those Bennets!"

Mrs. Hurst knocked and opened the door. "Caroline? I heard you down the hall."

"Close the door. I would not want the Bennets to decide to we need to leave tonight yet."

Mrs. Hurst stood with pursed lips. "It is most unfortunate that Charles had his head turned by her. He married her even with her lack of connections and horrid relations! But there is nothing we can do. It is no use carrying on this way or you will keep Charles and his inheritance away."

Miss Bingley turned on her sister. "His inheritance? Part of that inheritance is to support his sisters. Yet we are being tossed out of our home because of his wife. I rue the day I ever thought moving to the country would be a delightful change of scenery."

Mrs. Hurst smiled at her sister but worried for her felicity with her sister living with her and Mr. Hurst. They had a nice townhouse to be sure, but not enough room for three adults. Mrs. Hurst hoped Caroline would find a husband soon but with her on the shelf, who would be interested? She was not even sure Caroline's large dowry would attract suitors. Especially suiters that Caroline would find acceptable. Mrs. Hurst wished again that Caroline had not set her sights on Mr. Darcy and had instead taken the job of finding a husband seriously.

"I am excited to go back to town. You must be quite tired of country life as I am, Caroline. We should be around society and not this backwoods excuse for refinement. I cannot wait to leave."

Miss Bingley frowned at her sister. "You know I share the same sentiment. Just not the method of our leaving."

Mrs. Hurst turned to the door. "I want to leave early in the morning. Be ready."

Mrs. Hurst quit the room which left Miss Bingley to glare at her belongings.

~

Miss Bingley was barely civil during their departure the next day, but Mrs. Hurst knew the importance of staying on good terms with her brother and the influential Mr. Darcy.

Elizabeth and Jane beamed as their carriage rolled away from Netherfield for town. Elizabeth relished the pleasant quiet at Netherfield now that the termagants were gone.

She passed a pleasant afternoon reading while listening to Mary play the pianoforte. Her husband and Mr. Bingley were somewhere in the house. She hummed as she read and looked out the window but it was much too windy for walking.

"I SHOULD HAVE DONE this sooner. It is so nice to be in my home without fear of what Caroline will say or do next to embarrass me. Jane is much happier as well." Mr. Bingley smiled at his closest friend.

Mr. Darcy smirked.

"I know what you are going to say Fitzwilliam and you can keep it to yourself."

Mr. Darcy dropped his smirk. "What are you going to do about the rental in Meryton?"

"I am appalled at how they treated Elizabeth at Longbourn. For Mrs. Bennet to lock her in her bedroom! And her sisters, except Jane of course, were quite mean to her."

Mr. Darcy nodded. "I know. I wish Elizabeth had told me of this before you rented a house for them. They do not deserve it."

"They certainly do not. I cannot even kick them out as it would be foolish to pay rent on a place with no one living there." Mr. Bingley looked at his snifter of brandy.

"You could make it clear the lease will not be renewed. The Bennets have enough relatives between the Gardiners and the Phillips that they could be split between the two houses." Mr. Darcy leaned back in his chair.

Mr. Bingley stood and walked behind his desk. "What about Mary?"

Mr. Darcy tilted his head. "I do not recall Elizabeth mentioning that Mary harassed her. Mary should stay with one of us to improve her social graces. And her pianoforte playing."

"And her singing." Mr. Bingley raised an eyebrow and sat down behind his desk. "I shall write to their uncle, Mr. Gardiner. I will let him know I will not renew the lease on the rental."

"Do not forget to tell him why you are not renewing the lease." Mr. Darcy scowled as he remembered what Elizabeth had said about that time at Longbourn.

Mr. Bingley nodded. "Do not worry, Fitzwilliam. I will definitely make my displeasure known."

CHAPTER 38

It was another mild winter day, full of sunshine. Mr. Darcy accompanied Elizabeth on her walk, but they did not stray far from Netherfield. Elizabeth felt stupid because she was afraid to walk beyond Netherfield's gardens, but she could not reason away her fear. Instead, she would pretend nothing was wrong. Even though they never walked where she could not see Netherfield.

"I imagine you have walked more since marrying me, than you had before?" Elizabeth glanced at her husband, who she knew would much rather be riding. But he was here with her to combat her fear.

"You are correct. It does not mean that the activity is not unwelcome though."

They both stopped as a rabbit shot out from the brush. Mr. Darcy walked then turned when he realized Elizabeth was not beside him. She stood still on the path and shook.

Mr. Darcy walked the few steps back to her. "Elizabeth?" It was obvious the events had left their mark on her psyche.

"Fitzwilliam, I feel so stupid. I have never feared anything and now I am scared of a rabbit!"

Mr. Darcy wrapped his arms around Elizabeth. "It is not stupid at all. It was a frightening ordeal you went through. The more we walk the more confident you will become. Come, let us continue our walk."

Elizabeth wrapped her arm around his and they continued their walk. "I dislike being so scared."

"You have nothing to be ashamed about."

Elizabeth glanced at her husband. "Have you heard of what will happen to Mr. Collins?"

"A notice for the Winter Assizes went up in Meryton. Mr. Collins' trial will be held at the Assizes and his punishment determined then." Mr. Darcy looked at Elizabeth. "We will need to testify as witnesses."

Mr. Darcy worried the trial, the recounting of the events would make her fears even greater and undo any progress she had made.

"I will be glad when this is all over. It is odd to know a defendant in trial at the Assizes. We all read the Newgate Calendar as children. I am sure you did too."

Mr. Darcy nodded. "I believe it is a common reading for every household in England. A way to scare children into behaving."

"It does not seem to have worked with all."

They walked companionably for some time before Elizabeth spoke again. "I wonder what your aunt must think of Mr. Collins? I remember him stating that she had appointed the living at Hunsford parsonage to him?"

"Yes, she did. I do not know what she thinks of him now, but I know she does not like to be proven wrong." Mr. Darcy glanced at Elizabeth with a raised eyebrow.

The Winter Assizes for the Home Circuit was held at Hertford in the country Hertfordshire. It was but a 27 minute ride from Meryton to Hertford, but it felt much longer to Elizabeth's nerves. Mrs. Bennet and the other Bennet girls were in another coach. Mr. Gardiner, Jane and Mr. Bingley were in the Darcy's coach. They provided a hack for the former servants of Longbourn so they could testify to Mr. Collins' behavior.

Elizabeth had never attended an Assizes and had never wanted to. She could not understand the bloodlust in the many that did. They would attend the Assizes for the day then follow the prisoner's cart to Gallows Hill in Hertford to watch the hangings. Elizabeth shuddered and turned to the coach's window.

Mr. Darcy leaned over. "Are you cold? There is another blanket."

Elizabeth turned towards him. "I am not cold. I am just... I want Mr. Collins to admit what he did and face punishment, but I dislike the thought of the punishment being his death. That we, as witnesses are responsible for his transportation or hanging."

"Elizabeth...." Mr. Darcy squeezed Elizabeth's hand, "I want nothing less than death for him for what he did and attempted to do to you. It is not you or I that are putting him to death. It is his own actions."

"Indeed," said Mr. Gardiner from the other side of the coach, "that was well put, Mr. Darcy. Elizabeth, you are kind and caring which I am glad for, but in this case, it is for the betterment of society that men like Mr. Collins can no longer prey upon other women."

"Well said!" Mr. Bingley exclaimed. "I do not want him around Jane or anyone else I know. And it was his fault entirely for what transpired."

Elizabeth smiled, looked back at Mr. Darcy and squeezed his hand. She would get through this.

"Each case is only 30 minutes long." Mr. Darcy informed her. "Soon it will be over, and we can leave."

Elizabeth stilled. "Is that even enough time to hear from all the witnesses? That does not seem nearly enough time when someone's life hangs in the balance."

"There are so many cases to be heard each day at the Assizes so each case is moved along quickly." Mr. Gardiner frowned. "It does not seem like enough time to determine the fate of a man's life but it is what it is."

THE ASSIZES WERE HELD in the town hall. Tables, chairs and half walls were brought in to create the docks. The docks were separate holding areas for the public, witnesses and prisoners. The judge sat on a raised platform. There was not enough room for all the witnesses and for the public, so people moved in and out after each case. The public overflow would have to stand outside the makeshift courtroom, or even outdoors if it was a popular case.

Elizabeth stood next to Mr. Darcy and Jane as the procession of the judge, lawyers, local clergy, mayor and other important public figures marched in to the town hall. It looked that attending the Assizes was a popular entertainment by the crowd gathered. Elizabeth frowned and wished she could be anywhere else instead of having to relate to strangers what Mr. Collins had done to her.

The rest of the open seats on one side were for the public, with members of the upper class given first choice. They settled in their chairs and waited for the court to begin.

Jane leaned over to Elizabeth. "This room smells very nice. I did not think they would perfume it to hear cases. That seems rather odd."

Mr. Darcy leaned forward from the other side of Elizabeth. "You will not have the misfortune of being in this room all day. By the end of the day, I have heard the courtrooms have a unique smell from all the prisoners and public."

Elizabeth wrinkled her nose. She did not want to be here one bit, but was thankful Mr. Darcy was right beside her.

The judge walked into the courtroom as the Crier yelled. "Oyez, Oyez, Oyez! My lords the King's justices do strictly charge and command all manner of persons to keep silence, while the king's commissions of assize and nis prius, oyer and terminer, and general gaol-delivery for this county of Hertfordshire are openly read, upon pain of imprisonment.[1]"

Elizabeth swallowed and her breathing quickened. Jane held her other hand and squeezed.

The members of the jury were called one by one and sworn in by the marshal. The first prisoner was called in and brought up to the bar as his indictment was read. The proceedings moved quickly. It was so fascinating that despite her anxiety Elizabeth followed the proceedings, witness examinations and indictments and calmed. This was more intriguing than any play or book.

A disturbance at the back of the hall caused many to look behind them.

"Do you know who I am? Make way!"

CHAPTER 39

The court proceedings paused as a tall well-dressed woman entered the hall with a liveried servant walking behind her. The servant walked up the aisle, between the docks for the public and the witnesses to the opening for the public seats. All watched as the servant leaned down and spoke to someone seated in a chair at the front of the dock. That person stood and offered his chair. The grand woman walked past him with a slight nod of her head and then sat. The servant stood to the side of the chair.

Elizabeth shared a wide-eyed look with Jane and then turned to Mr. Darcy. His head was bowed, and he groaned. "Fitzwilliam, are you unwell?"

Mr. Darcy shook his head, raised it and looked at Elizabeth. She could tell by his narrowed eyes and pursed lips that he was quite unhappy. "That woman is the patroness whom Mr. Collins so often mentioned, Lady Catherine de Bourgh, who just so happens to be--"

"Your aunt!" Elizabeth looked again at the woman. She could see the woman's raised head and very fine hat from where she sat. "What is she doing here?"

"I fear she is here as a witness for Mr. Collins' defense."

Elizabeth's eyes widened. "Your aunt as his defense? Does she not know what he attempted to do to you?"

"She does because I wrote her."

Elizabeth was speechless.

"She did not send felicitations for our marriage. It was quite the opposite. I imagine this is her way to continue to show her displeasure with me."

Elizabeth stared at the woman at the front of the court proceedings. She could never imagine being so mean to one of her own relatives. What a horrid woman she must be.

The muttering and movements of the public slowly dwindled back down as the proceedings carried on as normal. It seemed like no time had passed before the Crier announced "Mr. William Collins."

Elizabeth jumped in her seat and turned to look at Mr. Collins as he entered. He had lost weight, his hair was stringy and greasy and his skin sallow. Elizabeth leaned back and into Mr. Darcy's side. Mr. Darcy wrapped his arm around her shoulders.

The Crier read off the Bill of Indictment. "The jurors of our sovereign lord the king upon their oath present that William Collins late of the parish of Meryton in the County of Hertfordshire not having God before his eyes but being moved and seduced by the instigation of the devil in the Reign of our Sovereign Lord George the Third, King of Great Britain, etc. with Force and Arms at the Parish aforesaid in the County aforesaid upon the Bennet family burglurously and felonously stole the Bennet's property and destroyed it, upon one Mrs. Elizabeth Darcy violently and felonously did assault with the intent to murder and did so felonously and maliciously intend to murder Mr. Fitzwilliam Darcy. Against the Peace of our said Lord the King, his Crown and Dignity and against the form of the Statute in such Case made and provided.[1]"

Lady Catherine de Bourgh stood and brought the mumblings in the courtroom to complete silence. "This is all a great falsehood and slander upon the good name of Mr. Collins whom I appointed as the parson of Hunsford. I demand you release this man and drop all charges at once."

The Crier gaped at her then turned to the bailiff and then to the judge.

The judge banged his gavel. "I will have silence in my courtroom. Madam ---"

She raised herself up to stand taller. "I am Lady Catherine de Bourgh."

"My apologies your Ladyship. You may be a witness for the prisoner at the appropriate time. Please be seated."

Lady Catherine scowled then sat back in her seat with a raised chin.

The judge nodded to the Clerk of the Arraigns who cleared his throat. "How sayest thou William Collins art thou guilty of the Felony and Theft whereof thou indicted or not guilty?"

Mr. Collins was not paying attention to the court proceedings. Instead he gaped at Lady Catherine de Bourgh.

The judge pounded his gavel. "Prisoner, answer the question!"

Mr. Collins answered. "N..n..not guilty."

"Culprit, how wilt thou be tried?"

"B..by God and my country."

"God send thee a good deliverance."

The Crier then spoke. "Oyez, Oyez, Oyez; My Lords the King's Justices strictly charge command all manner of persons to keep silence upon pain of imprisonment." He swept the gallery with a scowl and then continued. "Oyez, Oyez, Oyez; If any one can inform my Lords the King's Justices, the King's Sergeant, the King's Attorney General, of any treasons, murders, felonies, or misdemeanors, committed or done by the Prisoner at the Bar, let him come forth, and he shall be heard, for the Prisoner stands now at the Bar upon their deliverance; and all persons that are bound by recognizance to give evidence against the Prisoner at the Bar, let them come forth and give their evidence, or they will forfeit their recognizances.[2]"

The Council for the Crown spoke. "Gentlemen, I told you at first, I would make no appeal to your passions, nor shall I; I have told you the story as it was told to me; I shall call the Witnesses, and if they do, prove the case to your satisfaction, you will, I doubt not, find the Prisoner guilty. If they do not prove it, God forbid that an innocent person should suffer. It is our business to lay it fairly, candidly, and fully before you, and then in God's name, let the consequence follow.[3]"

Elizabeth squeezed Jane's and Mr. Darcy's hands. She gathered herself, stood and focused on Mr. Darcy's back as they walked out of their dock over to the Council for the Crown. Mr. Collins' case had the largest number of witnesses by far. The Council took their names and had them sit in the dock for witnesses until called.

Hill was called first. She trembled and was pale as a sheet. She answered the prosecution's questions but no one could hear her. The judge told her to speak up and then she shouted her answers to the amusement of the crowd.

It was a good thing she shouted as Lady Catherine de Bourgh interjected her opinion often. Especially when Hill stated that she saw Mr. Collins tear Elizabeth's dresses, and he told Hill to burn them.

"Poppycock!" Lady Catherine pounded her cane on the floor. "This is nothing but slander and lies. You should charge her!"

The judge glanced at Lady Catherine de Bourgh and scowled.

Mrs. Bennet then stood as a witness. She was too overwhelmed with the proceedings and did not carry on with histrionics when telling a story as she normally did. She stated what property was missing including furniture, clothing, personal items and especially her parent's portraitures.

Lady Catherine interjected. "This is all conjecture. A servant moved those items. You will most likely find them in storage."

The crowd guffawed.

Mrs. Bennet flushed.

The judge glanced at Lady Catherine and banged the gavel. "Silence."

Lady Catherine de Bourgh straightened her skirts.

Mr. Gardiner now stood as the executor of his brother-in-law's will and guardian of the family. He stated what he witnessed when he tried to do his duty and determine the family's finances.

Now it was the time Elizabeth had dreaded. They called her as a witness. Mr. Darcy squeezed her hand and told her everything would be fine. She walked up in front of the judge and jury, then turned to face the Crown's Council. She looked straight at the prosecutor, so as not to lose her nerve.

Elizabeth related her inability to claim one of her father's effects as Mr. Collins had locked his study even though the items inside were not part of the entailment of Longbourn. She teared as she told how the family went to Longbourn with the magistrate, but the study had been cleared of Mr. Bennet's effects and she had nothing of his. She took a deep breath and told of her walk that one day and the assault upon her person by Mr. Collins.

"This is a most slanderous falsehood!" Lady Catherine stood.

The judge turned. "Your ladyship, will you please sit down and be silent? Your time will come."

"There is outrageous harm being done to the reputation of Mr. Collins. I am great proficient at understanding people. I would not have placed Mr. Collins in the Hunsford parsonage if I thought he was capable of such vile acts as this girl just stated."

Mr. Darcy stood and scowled. "Lady Catherine de Bourgh, you have cast slanderous aspersions on my wife. She has not made up a story. Everything she has said is the truth. I came upon her during Mr. Collins' attack. You know I say nothing but the truth at all times and my wife is the same."

The crowd moved their heads back and forth between the two. To have two members of the upper class in court and arguing with each other was a momentous event that would be retold many times over.

"You cannot tell me Mr. Collins knew where you would walk in the country that day?" Lady Catherine asked Elizabeth.

Elizabeth stared at the prosecutor and did not answer until the prosecutor himself asked the same question. She frowned but answered. "I had walked the same path for a few days in a row."

"You expect us to believe Mr. Collins knew exactly where you would be? This is preposterous. It is a falsehood constructed by a girl angry that her family's home was entailed to Mr. Collins." Lady Catherine banged her cane on the floor.

Elizabeth flushed and pursed her lips. She looked at Mr. Darcy who opened his mouth, but it was not his voice she heard.

"It is all my fault! I am so sorry, Lizzy. I did not know he questioned me about your walks to hurt you!"

CHAPTER 40

The crowd gasped and uttered exclamations at Lydia's outburst. Elizabeth gaped at her sister, unable to comprehend what she had just heard.

The judge pounded the gavel. "Silence!"

The prosecution for the Crown motioned for Lydia to come up.

Elizabeth rushed from where she had stood in front of the judge to Mr. Darcy's arms. She breathed a sigh of relief.

The prosecution questioned Lydia regarding her outburst. Mr. Wickham had questioned Lydia during a trip to Meryton to look at rental houses.

Lydia had unintentionally told him all he needed to know to find Elizabeth.

That had been the key part of the events that had bothered Elizabeth. How had they known where she walked and when? Now, she knew they had been stalking her thanks to Lydia. Her youngest sister, flirted with the officers while she was still in mourning, and allowed Wickham to question her without realizing that no gentleman would break society's rules. Or Lydia had realized this fact, but did not care.

They released Lydia from questioning and she walked straight to Elizabeth. Her remorse and guilt seemed truthful. She begged Elizabeth to forgive her. Even though Elizabeth wanted to yell at her, she hugged her instead. What else could be done? Perhaps now Lydia had seen the error of her ways and would act with more introspection and propriety.

They called Mr. Darcy next. He relegated the events from his point of view, from coming upon Mr. Collins' assault on Elizabeth, to the duel with Mr. Wickham.

They excused Mr. Darcy, and it was now time to hear witnesses for the defense of the prisoner. The judge, the Crown's Council and the entire courtroom looked at Lady Catherine de Bourgh.

She stood and regally strode to the center aisle. She turned towards the judge, jury and prisoner dock. "Mr. Fitzwilliam Darcy is the son of my late sister Lady Anne Darcy of Pemberley in Derbyshire. I have known Mr. Darcy since he was a babe. He does not utter falsehoods."

Lady Catherine de Bourgh scowled at the sniveling Mr. Collins. She turned and proceeded out of the town hall to the pleading and crying of Mr. Collins.

The room exploded in a roar. All discussed the dramatic turn of events that had just occurred. The public congratulated themselves on having got into the hall for this case instead of being stuck outside.

Elizabeth sat next to Mr. Darcy in the witnesses' dock. She was glad she had not run afoul of Lady Catherine de Bourgh before. She could imagine the things that woman would have said to her regarding her marriage to her nephew, Mr. Darcy.

Mr. Collins continued to beg and plead for mercy in between screaming that the Lord would smite everyone that had cast aspersions upon his character.

The members of the jury were told to deliberate. Elizabeth leaned to the side and watched them talk amongst themselves. A few even stood and moved closer to the middle of the group. In no time at all, just a few minutes, they were done and had a verdict.

"Gentlemen, are you all agreed on your verdict?" said the Clerk of Arraigns.

"Yes."

"How say you, is Mr. William Collins guilty of these felonies whereof he stands indicted or not guilty?"

"Guilty."

Mr. Collins screamed.

The judge pounded his gavel. "The prisoner is found guilty. For felonies the punishment is transportation or death by hanging."

Elizabeth squeezed Mr. Darcy's hand. There was tension in the air as the room waited to find out whether Mr. Collins would live or die that day. Elizabeth did not know which one she wanted. She hated him for what he had done to her, her family and Mr. Darcy. But she did not want to be responsible for someone's death either.

"The prisoner, Mr. William Collins' punishment will be death by hanging today." The judge pounded the gavel.

They dragged Mr. Collins out crying and pleading.

Elizabeth exhaled and leaned forward with her head in her hands.

Mr. Darcy put his arm around her and squeezed. "It is over. Let us go. I do not want to stay for other cases. We have had enough for one day."

Elizabeth stood, and they walked arm in arm through the crowd and out of the town hall. They were somber for a man had been sentenced to death, a man they knew, their cousin. No matter how heinous his crimes, the sentencing of a man to die is no easy thing to witness.

Their mood was however far different from that of Mrs. Bennet and Lydia. They crowed they had known Mr. Collins would get what he deserved.

Lydia swung her arms with Kitty. "I can not wait to see Mr. Collins hang. I shall stick my tongue out at him and hope it is the last thing he sees!"

"I was ever so scared at the thought of going before a judge," said Mrs. Bennet, "in the Assizes. But I will have you know it was not as dreadful as I had been expecting. No, indeed! That horrible man got what was coming to him though."

"Mama!" Jane and Elizabeth called out.

"To steal our property and destroy it! He shall be hated in Hertfordshire forever more for what he did to us! And you, Elizabeth and Mr. Darcy." Mrs. Bennet glanced at her imposing son-in-law. "But, we shall never get our things back as Mr. Collins had them burned! My portraits of my parents! I will never see them again!"

"Mama, please!" Elizabeth pleaded.

"Calm yourself, Franny!" Mr. Gardiner grabbed Mrs. Bennet's arm. "This is not the place to discuss this." Mr. Gardiner steered her towards her coach.

"Oh, but this is a wonderful day brother, is it not? Mr. Collins will be hanged! He was not nice to you either. He had you banished from Longbourn! If only we could get Longbourn back. It should have never gone to that man in the first place."

Elizabeth turned away from her mother. "Why does she persist in carrying about in this manner?"

"I do not feel the celebration of punishment for the wrongs of a man is warranted in a case such as this," said Mary "even though he had greatly wronged many. We must be meek and be the better kind of woman, not preen and Lord our victories over our enemies."

"Yes, thank you Mary." Elizabeth shared a long look with her husband as they walked to their coach.

"Wait, where are you going?" Lydia ran to their group. "The hangings will not be 'till this afternoon. You cannot leave until you see Mr. Collins hang, especially you Elizabeth."

Elizabeth gaped at Lydia. "You may stay if you want, but I do not rejoice in the death of a man, no matter how much he wronged me."

Lydia made a face but then quickly composed herself after she glanced at Mr. Darcy. "Well leave if you shall, but I am going to stay. I know Mama will too. It is no less than Mr. Collins deserves." Lydia ran to where Mrs. Bennet stood accepting the attention of the crowd eager to hear a first-hand account of the horrors inflicted upon her by Mr. Collins.

They rode back to Netherfield without Mr. Gardiner. He had stayed to ensure the safety of his sister and nieces while they waited for, and watched the hangings.

~

ELIZABETH KNEW when her mother found out the lease on the rental in Meryton would not be renewed for another three months. Mrs. Bennet wrote both Jane and Elizabeth and asked if the estate she wanted had been purchased by Mr. Bingley. Both sisters threw the letters in the fire.

Her mother and younger sisters did come to visit them at Netherfield though thankfully not as often as Elizabeth had feared. Since neither Elizabeth nor Jane enjoyed gossip of the misfortunes of others, Mrs. Bennet did not enjoy her visits to Netherfield.

Lydia's short bout with remorse did not cause any lasting effect in her psyche. Mrs. Phillips wrote to Elizabeth and Jane separately and begged for them to take Lydia. She flirted with all the officers at Mrs. Phillips card parties and had caused a bout of fisticuffs at the last one. Lydia should have still been in mourning and not attended, but staying in the same house where officers were being entertained was too much for Lydia. Neither Jane nor Elizabeth relented. They were quite happy to not have Lydia at Netherfield. It was too bad for Kitty though, perhaps her behavior could be improved upon if she was away from Lydia.

Elizabeth and Mr. Darcy would not leave Hertfordshire until they knew the future of Longbourn. Elizabeth did not want it to leave her family if there was some way to reclaim it. She had grown up at Longbourn, knew every part of the grounds and had spent many a wonderful afternoon rambling about the countryside that surrounded it.

Finally, they received notice regarding the future of Longbourn.

CHAPTER 41

No other male relative of Mr. Bennet had been found. The estate of Longbourn had reverted to the Crown and would be sold at auction.

"Fitzwilliam, could we purchase Longbourn?" Elizabeth turned towards Mr. Darcy who sat at his desk in their bedchamber. "Not for us to live there, but for Mary. I do not want Longbourn to leave our family."

"I do not see why that would be a problem. You do not think Mary will find a husband?"

Elizabeth raised an eyebrow and gave Mr. Darcy a long look. "I would not want Mary to be a burden on our relatives. Especially when she is better behaved than the majority of them. Could we purchase Longbourn and give it to Mary?"

Mr. Darcy frowned. "She is an unmarried woman and cannot own property. We could put it in a trust for her use."

Elizabeth frowned. "No, I want it to be a home for the unmarried women in our family. For those who have not found a husband, nor are likely to, have a home. They will feel like a burden to their relatives."

"May I ask why Mary? How did she treat you when you were under lock and key for not accepting Mr. Collins' offer?"

Elizabeth turned and smiled at him. "I thank you for being my protector, but you need not worry. Mary and Jane were the only ones to not say a word to me about marrying Mr. Collins."

Mr. Darcy frowned. "We will purchase Longbourn and put it in a trust for the unmarried women of our relations."

Elizabeth smiled and sat on Mr. Darcy's lap. "Thank you. It would give me a great ease of mind to know that Mary will have a place to call home."

Mr. Darcy wrapped his arms around Elizabeth. "And what of your younger sisters?"

Elizabeth frowned, then smiled and laughed.

Mr. Darcy's eyebrow rose. "I fear to even ask."

"Mary will be the mistress of Longbourn, though the rest of my family, including Mama, will live with her!" Elizabeth laughed while she tried to speak. "She will have them reading Fordyce's Sermons every day!"

Mr. Darcy smiled.

"I cannot wait for this business to be over so we can finally go home to Pemberley." Elizabeth laid her head on Mr. Darcy's shoulder.

"WHAT?" Lydia turned from Mary who sat in a chair reading a book. "Mama! You cannot let her do this?"

Mary gazed at her youngest sister from where she sat in the chair closest to the fire. "I can and I shall. I am the mistress of Longbourn, Lydia and you are here only by my benevolence. If you do not want to follow my rules, you can leave and live with the Phillips'. If they will have you."

Lydia turned to Mary. "That is not nice! There is no reason for you to treat us so poorly! I do not want to read Fordyce's Sermons again!"

Mary put down her book and gazed at Lydia. "It is very important for every young woman to reflect upon our actions. We must make atonement for our past actions especially those in which we treated others uncommonly unworthy. I have had repeated opportunities of observing such behavior from you Lydia towards Mama and your sisters. Is it not our duty to make atonement to those we have wronged? By reflection and prayer, by leading a life of faith, contrition and charity the strictures of pride will be brought down. On the ruins will be the plain and modest, pleasing and graceful fabric of meekness[1]."

Lydia groaned and threw herself in a chair. "You can recall Fordyce's Sermons, Mary. Why do I need to read them when you can just quote them to me?"

Mary opened her book again. "Because if you do not do as I say, I can throw you out. You will have much less freedom, and a small bedchamber at the

Gardiner's house. They most probably do not even have room for that. You will have to share a room with the maid."

Lydia groaned and covered her face with her hands. She stomped on the floor. "This is not fair!"

Mary looked up at Lydia and then to Mrs. Bennet who pulled her embroidery thread too tight on the screen.

"Oh blazes! I tore another thread." Mrs. Bennet scowled at Mary. "It is quite rude how you treat me. To not even let me use the coach to visit Jane! I am being kept a prisoner in my own home!"

"But you are not, Mama, for it is not your home, it is mine. You know I told you that you could visit Jane after you write an apology to Elizabeth." Mary turned a page in her book. She had heard this same argument from her mother for several days now.

Lydia pouted at Mary from her chair. She knew better than to yell at Mary, not after she was sent to bed without supper like a little child. Blast that Mr. Darcy for hiring a footman for Longbourn.

Miss Bingley looked down at her plate and picked at the peas with her fork. She looked at the fork, then turned it back and forth as she watched the light reflect off no ornamentation. The plain silverware was nowhere near as grand as the kind used by Charles. It did not even hold a candle to the beautiful silverware at Pemberley.

Miss Bingley clenched the fork in her fist until her knuckles turned white. She still could not believe Mr. Darcy had married that country hoyden with no connections and mortifying relatives. How could he have done this to her? She had paid attention to him for years. She was the model of a perfect society wife who spoke several languages, could play the pianoforte, embroider a screen and have the utmost decorum. Why did Mr. Darcy turn her over for that ugly creature?

"I say there," the gentleman next to her leaned over, "are you planning to stab someone with your fork?" The man laughed to himself as Miss Bingley looked up and glared at her sister who sat next to her husband at the head of the table.

This had been one of many dinner parties her sister had thrown specifically to help Caroline find a husband. Miss Bingley did not want to become engaged though. She had only wanted Mr. Darcy and no one could ever measure up to that man. Louisa knew that, but after the first month in town her sister had mentioned that Miss Bingley needed to find a husband. Mr. Hurst had even gone so far as to mention that she visit other relatives. Blast that Elizabeth Bennet.

~

ELIZABETH SQUEEZED Mr. Darcy's hand. She looked out the carriage window eager to catch a sight of the magnificent Pemberley estate she had heard so much about. The park was very large and contained a great variety of ground. They had entered it in one of its lowest points and drove for some time through beautiful woods stretching over an expansive area. Elizabeth admired every spot and point of view. She could not wait to fully explore the grounds.

They gradually ascended and then found themselves at the top of a small hill where the woodland area ended, and Pemberley's beautiful facade came into view. Pemberley was situated on the opposite side of a pond. It was a large stone building rising high above the ground and backed by a ridge of high woody hills. Elizabeth was delighted. She was taken aback by the beauty and the fact that she was mistress of Pemberley.

"What are your thoughts of Pemberley? Do you like it?"

Elizabeth could barely tear her eyes from the view, but she did and gazed at her husband. "I do Fitzwilliam. I dearly love it. Anywhere is perfect though, if I am with you."

Mr. Darcy returned her smile. The coach rolled onwards to their home as Mr. Darcy leaned in to kiss Elizabeth.

The End

Thank you for reading! View Bella Breen's catalog of books.

For my steamy Mr. Darcy and Elizabeth stories view my Demi Monde books.

If you would like to know when I release a new book, and have a secret sale just for my newsletter subscribers, sign up for my newsletter. Yes, please, sign me up!

ENDNOTES

CHAPTER 38

1. Baltimore, Frederick Calvert. The Trial of Frederick Calvert, Esq.: Baron of Baltimore, in the Kingdom of Ireland for a Rape On the Body of Sarah Woodcock, and of Eliz. Griffinburg, and Ann Harvey, Otherwise Darby As Accessaries Before the Fact for Procuring, Aiding and Abetting Him in Committing the Said Rape. At the Assizes Held At Kingston, for the County of Surry On Saturday, the 26th of March 1768 Before the Hon. Sir Sydney Stafford Smythe, Knt .. Edinburgh: Printed for J. Balfour, 1768.

CHAPTER 39

1. Baltimore, Frederick Calvert. The Trial of Frederick Calvert, Esq.: Baron of Baltimore, in the Kingdom of Ireland for a Rape On the Body of Sarah Woodcock, and of Eliz. Griffinburg, and Ann Harvey, Otherwise Darby As Accessaries Before the Fact for Procuring, Aiding and Abetting Him in Committing the Said Rape. At the Assizes Held At Kingston, for the County of Surry On Saturday, the 26th of March 1768 Before the Hon. Sir Sydney Stafford Smythe, Knt .. Edinburgh: Printed for J. Balfour, 1768.
2. Baltimore, Frederick Calvert. The Trial of Frederick Calvert, Esq.: Baron of Baltimore, in the Kingdom of Ireland for a Rape On the Body of Sarah Woodcock, and of Eliz. Griffinburg, and Ann Harvey, Otherwise Darby As Acces-

saries Before the Fact for Procuring, Aiding and Abetting Him in Committing the Said Rape. At the Assizes Held At Kingston, for the County of Surry On Saturday, the 26th of March 1768 Before the Hon. Sir Sydney Stafford Smythe, Knt .. Edinburgh: Printed for J. Balfour, 1768.

3. Baltimore, Frederick Calvert. The Trial of Frederick Calvert, Esq.: Baron of Baltimore, in the Kingdom of Ireland for a Rape On the Body of Sarah Woodcock, and of Eliz. Griffinburg, and Ann Harvey, Otherwise Darby As Accessaries Before the Fact for Procuring, Aiding and Abetting Him in Committing the Said Rape. At the Assizes Held At Kingston, for the County of Surry On Saturday, the 26th of March 1768 Before the Hon. Sir Sydney Stafford Smythe, Knt .. Edinburgh: Printed for J. Balfour, 1768.

CHAPTER 41

1. Fordyce, James. Sermons to Young Women: In Two Volumes. By James Fordyce, D.D. The fourth edition, with additions and alterations. . Dublin: printed for J. Sheppard, 1766.

Made in the USA
Monee, IL
12 July 2023

38960562R00225